"I need a place to stay. Do you know anyone who has an apartment around here?" she asked.

Had Rona read about his job in the paper? The image of his boathouse apartment flashed in his mind, and Nick bit his tongue to control the offer, sensing it was a bad idea. He'd already come on too fast. "Not offhand, but I'll keep my ears open."

He fiddled with his paper napkin, hounded by the desire to be honest about the job opening with room and board. He liked her, that was true, but could she handle Gary? He wanted to do what was best for his son. He'd be wise to give himself time to know her better.

"Time's up." She looked disappointed as she slipped her mug onto the empty muffin plate. "I'd better get back to my shift before Bernie fires me on my second day."

Nick managed a grin but had to fight from praying for that exact thing to happen.

Books by Gail Gaymer Martin

Love Inspired

Upon a Midnight Clear #117
Secrets of the Heart #147
A Love for Safekeeping #161
*Loving Treasures #177
*Loving Hearts #199
Easter Blessings #202
 "The Butterfly Garden"
The Harvest #223
 "All Good Gifts"

*Loving Ways #231
*Loving Care #239
Adam's Promise #259
*Loving Promises #291
*Loving Feelings #303
*Loving Tenderness #323
In His Eyes #361
With Christmas in His Heart #373
In His Dreams #407
Family in His Heart #427

Steeple Hill Books

The Christmas Kite
Finding Christmas
That Christmas Feeling
 "Christmas Moon"

*Loving

GAIL GAYMER MARTIN

says when friends talk about events in their lives, they often stop short and ask, "Will this be in your next novel?" Gail only smiles, because sometimes they are. Gail feels privileged to write stories that honor the Lord and touch people's hearts.

With forty contracted books, Gail is a multi-award-winning author published in fiction and nonfiction. Her novels have received numerous national awards, and she has over a million books in print.

Gail, cofounder of American Christian Fiction Writers, lives in Michigan with her husband, Bob. When not behind her computer, she enjoys a busy life—traveling, presenting workshops at conferences, speaking at churches and libraries, and singing as a soloist and as a member of her church choir where she also plays handbells and hand chimes. She also sings with one of the finest Christian chorales in Michigan, the Detroit Lutheran Singers. To learn more about her, visit her Web site at www.gailmartin.com. Write to Gail at P.O. Box 760063, Lathrup Village, MI 48076 or at authorgailmartin@aol.com. She enjoys hearing from readers.

Family in His Heart
Gail Gaymer Martin

Steeple
Hill®

Published by Steeple Hill Books™

STEEPLE HILL BOOKS

Steeple
Hill®

ISBN-13: 978-0-373-87463-7
ISBN-10:   0-373-87463-4

FAMILY IN HIS HEART

Copyright © 2008 by Gail Gaymer Martin

All rights reserved. Except for use in any review, the reproduction
or utilization of this work in whole or in part in any form by any
electronic, mechanical or other means, now known or hereafter
invented, including xerography, photocopying and recording, or in
any information storage or retrieval system, is forbidden without
the written permission of the editorial office, Steeple Hill Books,
233 Broadway, New York, NY 10279 U.S.A.

This is a work of fiction. Names, characters, places and incidents are
either the product of the author's imagination or are used fictitiously, and
any resemblance to actual persons, living or dead, business establishments,
events or locales is entirely coincidental.

This edition published by arrangement with Steeple Hill Books.

® and TM are trademarks of Steeple Hill Books, used under license.
Trademarks indicated with ® are registered in the United States Patent
and Trademark Office, the Canadian Trade Marks Office and in other
countries.

www.SteepleHill.com

Printed in U.S.A.

Do not forget the things your eyes have seen
or let them slip from your heart as long as you live.
Teach them to your children
and to their children after them.

—*Deuteronomy* 4:9

Dedication and Acknowledgments

To my sister, Jan Hoffman,
who was my research companion for this book.

Thank to Capt. James Shutt of Dream Seaker
Chapters who agreed to a spur of the moment
three-hour tour of the Les Cheneaux Islands and
provided me with tremendous information.
If I erred or distorted facts, accept it as an
author's prerogative.

Thanks also to Officer Troy Johnston of the
Mackinac County Sheriff's Department in
St. Ignace for his assistance.

I am very grateful to the booksellers at Safe Harbor
Books and The Book Nook for welcoming me,
and to the Les Cheneaux Community Library and
to Betty Bailey and her husband at the Drummond
Island Tourism Association information center.

Chapter One

"Oh, no!"

The cry jarred Rona Meyers from her contemplation too late to escape the hot liquid that seeped through her pant leg as the waitress hit the floor along with the silverware. With customers' exclamations ringing in her ears, Rona scooted from the bench to help with the mess, but a man in a nearby booth had scrambled up first.

Of all the men present, he'd been the only one to come to the waitress's rescue and Rona admired the man's gallantry. The more she looked, the more she admired him. His rugged handsomeness, his tanned face and his brawny stature caused him to stand out among the others present.

With his help, the waitress rose, her face glowing the color of a ripening apple while she still clutched the empty tray. With tears rolling down her cheeks, she ran behind the counter and through the door into the kitchen, leaving behind the mess of broken china and uneaten food.

Feeling distress for the young woman, Rona watched the intriguing man return to his booth before focusing on the dark spots soiling her otherwise clean beige pants. She grasped a paper napkin and daubed the stain, grateful the coffee had only been hot and not scalding.

When she looked up, the gentleman was eyeing her as if to acknowledge she'd tried to help the waitress, too. Rona gave him a feeble grin and looked away, uneasy with his obvious attention and hoping he hadn't noticed her gaping at him.

The kitchen door remained closed and Rona watched it to see what would happen now. Would the young woman regain her composure and return to clean up the mess, or would she sulk for a while in the back room?

Rona had experienced the same feelings. Being a waitress wasn't easy. The recollection settled into her mind—the hard work, low wages and the sometimes tip-less tables that she'd found so discouraging.

Ridding herself of the memory, Rona gazed out the window at the sun glinting against Lake Huron on Michigan's north shore. The muted silvery gold streak rippled like the yellow line on the highway through the rain—or through tears.

A short distance across the lake one of the Les Cheneaux Islands rose above the water, its shoreline thick with trees and dotted by an occasional home— large homes with elaborate two-storied boathouses. She'd noticed the island on trips to the area with her friend Janie, who'd come to Hessel to visit her aunt. The memory had remained and had drawn her back here now when she needed to get away from her disturbing life.

Distant voices came from the kitchen; Rona watched the door, but the voices only grew louder. She looked away and noticed the stranger watching her again. He sent her a wide smile that made his eyes crinkle. His hair looked tousled. If he'd stop looking at her, she would enjoy looking at him.

Finally the kitchen voices silenced. The door swung open and a tall, lanky man charged behind the counter pulling meals from the serving window and scanning the crowded tables. He studied the tickets, then gave a nod as if he'd discovered his answer and slid the dishes up his arm and headed to a table across the room. He wore an apron, so she assumed he was a cook. This appearance brought an obvious question into her head. Where was the waitress?

Rona followed the man's journey with her eyes, watching him hand over the dishes with skill, then head back toward the kitchen. As he passed, the good-looking man's hand shot out and nabbed the cook.

Curious, she leaned closer, hoping to hear the conversation, but his soft voice didn't carry.

The cook's did.

"She quit, Nick," he said, his arm swinging toward the kitchen door. "Walked out the back door screaming that she hated the job. Now I'm really shorthanded. No busboy today, either."

Shorthanded. The word skittered down Rona's spine, worked its way into her head. Her throat tightened with the words that formed in her mind.

Nick gave the cook's arm a pat along with what

appeared to be a look of encouragement, then his gaze captured hers again and her stomach twisted.

Nick reminded her of a lumberjack. She could picture his broad shoulders and wide chest pivoting as his powerful arms swung an ax. She couldn't help but think of Michigan's legendary lumberman Paul Bunyan. The name Nick "Bunyan" came to mind and she grinned.

When she focused, Nick Bunyan was smiling back at her. She wanted to sink into her seat. Instead, she turned her eyes on the cook as he headed her way.

"Sir," she said, keeping her voice low while hoping he heard her.

The cook glanced at her without really looking. "I'll get your bill in a minute. I'm short a waitress."

Though she'd tried to hold them back, her need caused words to fly from her mouth. "I've done waitressing."

Her comment jerked him to a stop. "You what?"

"I've been a waitress. If you need someone, I'll give you a hand."

His surprised look shrunk to a frown. "You're willing to fill in for Gerri? You're pulling my leg."

"No. I'm new in town and need a job. One day's work is better than nothing." Her heart rose to her throat.

His jaw sagged as he seemed to contemplate what she'd said.

Looking at his expression, she wondered why she'd opened her mouth. Waitressing wasn't her favorite work, but if he liked her, it could mean a start in the new town. She'd look for something more suitable after she had settled. Her meager bank account wouldn't last forever.

"Butcher," he said.

"Butcher?"

"My name. Bernie Butcher. Quite a mouthful, don't you think?" He motioned for her to follow without giving her a moment to introduce herself.

Rona grabbed her shoulder bag, rose and dropped the paper napkin on the table. She stepped around the mess on the floor, not wanting to find herself flattened against the abandoned burger and ketchup-laden fries.

The kitchen door had begun to swing close, but she caught it and stepped inside, assailed by the odor of grease and heat from the griddle and frier.

Bernie—Mr. Butcher—gestured her across the room to a doorway. He followed, pushing open the door of a small storage area. "Put your belongings in here and grab an apron."

She tucked her handbag into a niche and pulled an apron from a hook, then tied it around her waist. As she turned back and reached for the doorknob, she spotted a floor plan of the Harbor Inn's seating arrangement and table stations. She studied it a moment, hoping she could remember which table was which.

While pride railed her for offering to help, common sense led her to the cook rather than following Gerri's path and escaping out the door. "By the way, my name's—"

"Food's up for table six." He pointed to the dishes lining the warming window.

Her head whirling, she read the ticket, recalled the floor plan and carried the food to the table she hoped was number six. As she approached, the diners' expressions let her know she'd made a good guess.

"Here you go," she said, balancing the plates as she removed them from her arm. "I'm sorry for the wait." She eyed their near empty cups. "I'll be right back with fresh coffee and some ketchup."

The customers nodded and dove into their food while she scurried away to bring back the items. Her waitress skills popped into her consciousness. She refreshed their coffee, then put on a new pot and headed for two new arrivals.

When she placed their order, she grabbed the next ticket. Table three. The floor plan shot into her mind. Nick Bunyan. She gazed at the whitefish sandwich with a dollop of slaw on the side. Healthier than fries or a greasy burger. She pictured him swinging the ax as her unsteady hand grasped the plate.

Rona avoided his gaze as she crossed the floor to him, realizing someone had cleaned up the fallen mess. She slid the plate in front of him. "I'll bring you a refill. Decaf or regular?"

"Regular, and nice job." He tilted his head toward the kitchen.

His comment caught her off guard. "Thanks," she said, trying to avoid his eyes. But he touched her arm and she had to look.

He gave her a faint smile. "Black."

Black? The word hung in the air until she remembered the coffee. "I'll be right back." His grin unsettled her, though she knew she was being silly. Most people in a small town recognized a stranger and she was a stranger.

After filling his cup, she took other orders and refreshed drinks, avoiding him; but drawn by curiosity, she couldn't help but glance his way. She saw him sipping the coffee and scanning a newspaper.

His gaze lifted from the paper to hers.

He'd caught her gaping again. Rona looked away as if she hadn't noticed. She'd come to Michigan's upper peninsula to get away from her past and keep a low profile, but she hadn't done a very good job today. She'd lived so much on the edge of stress, tension knotted in her again.

Foolish. He was a good-looking man, a kind man, she reminded herself. He meant nothing by his stare. New in town, she was a curiosity.

She concentrated on her work, took orders and bussed tables, wondering why Butcher or Bernie, whatever she was supposed to call him, hadn't hired more help. She would certainly earn her wage today— whatever it was. She'd forgotten to ask.

Rona zipped past Nick and pushed a utility cart filled with dirty dishes through the kitchen door. The lunch crowd had slowed and she stood a moment to get her bearings.

Bernie pulled out a basket of fries to drain and headed her way. "You're a lifesaver." He wiped his hand on his apron and stuck it out toward her. "And a good one."

"Thank you." She grinned at his overdone welcome. "I'm Rona Meyers, in case you want to know who's worked here for the last two hours."

"Sorry." He lowered his head as if realizing what he'd done. "I own the place and when things go wrong, I lose my cool. My busboy called in sick and then Gerri quit. What I need is good steady help."

She could be good steady help, but he didn't know

her and she was certain he wouldn't hire a stranger. She only nodded at his complaints.

"Mandy should be here in another hour, and Jimmy'll bus."

"Then I'll keep going until someone shows up."

He'd turned away, and she was left feeling empty again. For two hours she'd had a purpose, even if it was only waitressing, but it appeared that in a couple of hours, it would be over. She'd find work somewhere.

Rona snatched an empty cart, pulled it into the dining room and parked it beside the counter, then grabbed the coffeepot. When she turned, she felt her heart sink a little. Nick's table was empty, but he'd left her a five dollar tip—more than she deserved.

What did she care except he'd added a little excitement to her life. She grimaced, recalling excitement was what she wanted to escape.

The next hour flew past, and when a cute blond woman came in through the back door, Rona assumed she was Mandy. The woman gave her a strange look as if to ask what was she doing in the kitchen.

"Gerri quit," Bernie said, apparently noticing her questioning look.

"Oh." She moved closer. "You're the new waitress?"

She wished. "I'm Rona. Just filling in."

Her scowl turned to a smile as she extended her hand. "I'm Mandy."

Rona shook her hand, then glanced at the clock. "Guess I can get on my way." She eyed Bernie, waiting for him to offer to pay her.

Instead, he pointed toward the warmer. "Can you catch that?"

She scooted back through the door, grabbed the two fish platters, then stopped in her tracks. After only an hour, Nick had returned. Rona veered in the other direction and set the plates in front of two men deep in conversation.

Before she took another step, Nick flagged her to his table. "Mandy will catch your order. She'll be out in a moment."

"I'd like to talk with you for a minute if you don't mind."

A frown tightened her forehead. "Me?" She poked her index finger against her chest, sensing he was coming on to her.

He nodded. "When you're finished."

She eyed him a moment. "If you think—"

"I'm not thinking anything."

He grinned and her concern eased, but it didn't stop her questions. What did he want? Why had he come back?

His good looks melded with her curiosity and she realized she'd assumed the negative without using good sense. She'd come here to escape her unhappy life and now she realized she'd brought the fears along with her.

Without answering him, Rona shot back into the kitchen, longing to know what the man wanted, but thinking it might be best to leave through the back door. Before Bernie asked her to do anything else, she slipped off her apron, strode to the storage room and hung it on the hook where she'd found it. She pulled her shoulder bag from the niche and drew in a deep breath.

Gaining composure, Rona walked back into the

kitchen. "I'm leaving," she said, waiting for Bernie to acknowledge her.

He finally glanced at the wall clock, then turned his head to look at her. "We're still short help. Why don't you stick around until five."

"Until five?" If staying meant the possibility of being offered the job, she needed to use wisdom. "Okay."

"Family here?" He shuffled his feet as if he were hedging.

"No family. I knew the Baileys who live in Hessel. It was years ago, when I was a kid, and I always had good memories of the Les Cheneaux area."

"When you were a kid?"

He studied her as if wondering why it had taken her so long to return to the area. At thirty-nine, she was far from a kid.

His jaw twitched as his eyebrows raised. "You mean Sam and Shirley Bailey?"

She nodded.

"Sam died last year, but Shirley's still in the same place."

Sam died. She remembered the friendly man who had been Janie's grandfather.

"You're only just visitin' then."

Now Rona shuffled her feet as uncertainty winged its way into her thoughts, but she'd made a life change and she would honor her plans. "I'm staying."

"You did a good job today pinch-hittin' like that." He shuffled his feet again. "Lookin' for work?"

His question raised her spirits. She gave a half-hearted shrug. "Actually, yes, but—"

"I'd like you to stay on. You worked hard and I

respect that." He smiled a toothy grin. "Plus, you surprised me making that offer to help and I surprised myself by accepting it. I don't know you from Adam."

She couldn't help but grin back. "I saw you were in a bind."

"I can give you six dollars an hour plus your tips," he said, shifting closer and keeping his volume just above a whisper. "I know that's not a fortune, but we have good tippers around here. For good service, that is."

She pictured Nick's five dollar tip. Six dollars an hour. Good tips. She remembered working for two-seventy-five plus tips. Rona did a quick calculation. Not a bad wage until she found something better. "I can give it a try." She paused knowing she had to be honest. "But if something better comes along, I make no guarantees."

He pondered her comment, probably knowing that not much else was available around the area. "You got yourself a deal." He stuck out his hand and gave hers a shake.

Bernie held up a finger. "I'll get you an application." He strode into the storage room and out again with the forms. "You can sit at a table and fill these out and, while you're at it, grab a bite to eat. I imagine you're hungry." He handed her the papers.

Sit at a table. So much for her back-door escape, and by now she didn't want to. She was hungry and a free meal sounded good. She ordered a whitefish sandwich—Nick's had looked good earlier in the day—then poured herself a cup of coffee and headed into the dining room.

Her gaze drifted to Nick, who had once again focused on the newspaper, sipping a cup of coffee that

Mandy must have brought to him. He was leaning his shoulder against the wall and she guessed he was waiting for her. She still hadn't figured out the reason he wanted to talk to her. She eyed him, then decided she might as well get it over with.

Rona bit her lips, knowing she was lying to herself. Getting it over with had nothing to do with her motivation. The man had captured her interest. Still she didn't want the guy to get the wrong idea.

Grasping the application and her coffee mug, she ambled to his table vacillating between interest and indecision. "Sorry." She waved the forms toward him and motioned to an empty seat. "Bernie asked me to fill out these forms so I'll sit—"

"You can fill them out here." He patted the space across from him. "I don't bite."

Her old uneasiness soared into her chest. He said he didn't bite, but she was too gullible. Even her own brother had conned her into making a decision she lived to regret. She knew her brother, but what did she know about Nick? Wavering with indecision, Rona could feel the stress in her face.

"Please," he said, his tone warm and genial.

She slid her cup onto the table and placed the application farther away, fearing she would stain them with her coffee. Her hands felt unsteady as she settled onto the chair.

"Fish sandwich's ready."

Hearing the voice, she turned and saw Bernie slide her dinner under the warmer. She halted Nick with her index finger and hurried to the serving window for her sandwich.

When she'd settled back on the chair, Nick gave the bun a coy grin. "Looks familiar."

His lighthearted tone brightened her spirit. "You had one earlier, I know. It looked good."

"It was." He gazed at her and she felt heat rise up her neck. Get a grip, she told herself, embarrassed that she'd allowed this stranger to wheedle his way into her life. She'd been duped before and though he said he wasn't thinking anything, how could she trust him? Maybe he was trying to pick her up. What kind of woman did he think she was? She'd always been too trusting, too unsuspecting, and it was time to change. She steadied herself and peered into his eyes. "I don't understand why you want to talk with me."

"I don't, either," he said, the same crooked grin spreading to his lips. "I'm curious, I guess."

"Curious?" His words skittered up her spine. "About what?"

"About you. What made you volunteer to wait tables? I've seen waitresses blow their corks and dart off, but I've never seen a customer stand up and take over."

"I've worked as a waitress." She felt the heat in her cheeks deepen. "Are you telling me you came back here because you were curious?"

His gaze drifted out the window, then back to her. "My son has track practice and I'm waiting for him."

Son. Then he was married. Embarrassed at her presumption, she lowered her eyes to his left hand. No ring. Did lumberjacks wear rings?

"You're a good dad to pick up your son from school." Nick's mouth twisted.

She'd never had her dad pick her up from anywhere, but then she'd been grateful he didn't. So often he was drunk.

"He doesn't have his runabout today and we live on the island." He tilted his head toward the window.

She followed his nod toward the island across the lake, filled with lovely houses bordered by acres of thickly wooded land. Privacy. Elegance.

"I was at a contractor's meeting in town and it was convenient." He gazed out the window toward the water and the look on his face made her wonder.

Convenient? She sensed he was dismissing her "good father" comment. "It's still nice." Rona pulled her gaze from the window back to him, her memory drifting back to an earlier comment. "You had a contractor's meeting. Then, you're in construction?"

He fingered his coffee mug. "Yes, and I own a resort on Drummond Island, up the road a few miles."

Construction, owns a resort—the man had to be wealthy. Her earlier lumberjack image vanished and she winced at her simplistic perception.

Her focus lowered to the table and the job application. For some reason she felt guilty. "I guessed you for a lumberjack."

He chuckled. "No, but my family once owned a logging company years ago." He offered her his hand. "My name's Nick Thornton."

Thornton. She felt another grin settle on her face. So much for Bunyan. She grasped his fingers. "I'm Rona Meyers."

He studied her face while she waited for him to say something. Anything.

Finally he gestured to the forms she'd pushed against the wall. "Job application?" His expression had changed so quickly to a frown.

She studied him without responding. His smile didn't return. "I need a job and Bernie offered. I figured I'd take it until something else comes along."

He drew back, his scowl deepening.

The look threw her. What did he care? "I was honest with Bernie. I told him no guarantee. He still offered me work as long as I want. I don't suppose I'll find much else in a small town like this, anyway."

He shifted her application form with his index finger. "There's work if you know where to look."

She studied his face, waiting for him to continue.

Silence fell between them again until she felt forced to speak. "Where should I look?"

"At me."

"At you?" She enjoyed looking at him. He had a great smile, good looks and a playful personality—if she felt like playing games, which she didn't right now. "What does that mean?"

"Doesn't matter. It's too late. You've found your own job." He lifted a newspaper from the chair beside him and slid it on the table, glanced at his watch and rose. "Gary's probably waiting. I'd better get."

He dropped two dollars on the table and took a step away before pivoting to face her again. "Nice to meet you, Rona," he said, walking backward.

She watched him swing through the front door and felt very alone. He appeared outside the window, crossed the street and headed along the sidewalk beside the marina. Then he vanished from her sight.

The application lay beside her hand, and she eyed it while her mind soared back to her situation in East-pointe when she'd been so naive. She'd had a number of bad relationships and now, with maturity, she was trying to decipher why she'd had such poor judgment. She trusted people too easily—that had been her discovery. The memory edged against her heart and the loneliness grew. She'd come here, knowing no one, really. Shirley Bailey probably wouldn't remember her.

Her coffee had cooled, but she took a last drink, trying to focus on her new life here in Les Cheneaux area—in Hessel. When the desolate feeling passed, she shifted her attention from the application to the newspaper.

Drawing it closer, she turned it to face her. Odd. Nick had left it open to employment ads. She skimmed the list until she spotted Nick's name. Her pulse tripped as she read the ad.

Housekeeper needed on Marquette Island.
Transportation provided. Good pay.
Room and board.
Contact Nick Thornton.

Transportation provided? With no bridge or ferry, that made sense. She studied his telephone number while her heart sank. Room and board. Good pay and an island. She'd be safer there.

But she didn't know Nick Thornton. Could she trust him? She'd be alone on an island with a man she didn't know. She rubbed her temples, then grinned. Could she trust herself?

Chapter Two

Nick pulled alongside the high school and watched the building. He liked to be on time. Gary had little patience and he tried not to stir up any more animosity than was necessary.

Kids were like that. They hated their parents once they reached their teens. Nick often wished he could ship Gary away to a farm and then bring him back when he'd become an adult and learned civility, patience and hopefully some love.

Fighting his son to live his Christian morals and values had gone by the wayside. Lately, Nick struggled to communicate about anything with Gary. He wondered if his wife hadn't died would Gary be different? Jill. Her image flashed through his mind along with guilt-laden memories. He stifled the vision before it got hold of him again.

The May sun beat against the window and Nick rolled down the pane to let the breeze drift in. The earth smelled pungent as if the winter's debris had revitalized the soil, making everything ready to grow. How often had he wished he could be revitalized that simply.

Revitalized. He pictured Rona, the woman at the restaurant. Now that was energy. She darted from one station to the next, pouring coffee, bussing tables and taking orders without a hitch—a bundle of the cutest energy he'd ever seen.

He could see her straight honey-colored hair bouncing against her shoulders, the sweep of the wave that tucked beneath her chin when she tilted her head. And those eyes, as gray as a stormy sky but with a hint of sunshine behind the clouds.

Nick snorted at his flowery rumination. What was he doing thinking of a stranger at the Harbor Inn? He needed a woman muddling his mind like he needed another belligerent son in his life. What he really needed was a housekeeper. Had he known she was looking for work he'd have told her about the job right away, stranger or not. He was desperate.

A breeze drifted in, bringing the scent of freshly mowed grass. He turned toward the school again and saw Gary meandering around the back of the building, his arm wrapped around a girl encased in the tightest jeans Nick had ever seen and a knit top that exposed more than it covered.

He shook his head, disgusted and saddened with today's morals. As if he hadn't noticed him, Gary leaned against a tree, nestled the girl into his arms and planted a kiss against her mouth. Nick tooted the car horn, hoping to end the public display.

At first, Gary didn't move, then finally rolled his

shoulders from the tree trunk, eased away from the young woman and ambled toward the SUV.

Nick rested his arm against the window frame and watched him amble nearer. "I've been waiting."

"I'm not going home. I forgot to tell you."

The young woman adhered to his side like a static-charged balloon. "Hi, Mr. Thornton," she murmured.

"Hi," he said, giving her a glance but not remembering her name—if he'd ever known it. "Gary, you should have told me. I've been hanging around town waiting for you. Better yet, you should have asked. What's up?"

Gary's face twisted to a sneer. "I'm going to Phil's. We have some things to do."

"What kind of things?"

"Dad, get off my back. Things."

Nick's body stiffened. "Please be more respectful, Gary. What kind of things? Studying?"

"Yah, studying."

The girl snickered and nestled closer against his side.

Studying held about as much reality as cleaning his room. "It's a school night and I'm not coming back to pick you up."

"Phil'll bring me home or I can spend the night."

"No, you can't. I want you home."

Gary slapped the car roof. "Come on, Dad. I'm not six anymore. I'm sixteen."

"That's right, and when you're twenty-one and earning your own living, you can stay out as long as you want." Nick's jaw tightened. "You'll be home by nine."

Gary scowled. "Ten."

"Okay, ten, but no later."

Gary drew back, lifted a hand and walked away.

Nick pondered the gesture as his son strode away from the SUV. Had it been a goodbye wave or an I-don't-want-to-hear-this-anymore gesture.

Nick fell back against the seat, feeling the warm breeze but forgetting the fresh scent and hopeful sense of something new he'd had earlier. He and Gary had become an old argument for the past two years. The first year after Jill's death had been one of silence. The last two had been years when silence would have been a gift.

His shoulders slumped as he pulled away. If he didn't love his son so much, he wouldn't care, but Gary was all he had now, his purpose for waking in the morning. With Jill gone—the word made him cringe—life had changed, and despite their rough times, his life had not just faded but died with her. He woke in the morning, ran his businesses, arrived home to be with his distant son and went to bed, wishing they'd never gone waterskiing that ill-fated day, wishing he'd never looked back at Jill.

The sunlight blurred against the hood of his SUV and he brushed the tears away with the back of his hand. He'd lost the sense of family. He'd become alienated from his son. Time to make changes. He needed to do something about his relationship with Gary. What, he didn't know, but he hoped the Lord would guide him. He and Gary had to come to an understanding, at least a tolerable existence, and Nick knew he had to live again.

A voice sounded in his head—Rona Meyers, a

feminine powerhouse. Maybe he could learn something about life from her. He'd seen those stormy eyes tinged with the hint of sunny hope. He needed hope and he definitely needed energy.

The late afternoon sun streaked across the lake as Rona exited the Harbor Inn the way she'd come in that afternoon.

She headed for her car, then stopped and looked back at the brick-red clapboard building with wide windows, letting reality sink in. She worked here.

The difference between Harbor Inn and the last café she'd worked struck her. Walking on the plank floor all day at Harbor Inn had been easier than the typical city-diner slab floor covered by tile or cheap carpet. Harbor Inn had a homey feeling. People knew people. They talked and joked. And if she needed anything right now, it was a sense of home.

She ambled past her car, drawn by the lulling roll of the lake. Small fishing boats lined the harbor along with private speedboats to carry passengers from the mainland to their homes on the islands—thirty-six islands, she'd learned from Bernie when he'd accepted her application and taken a minute to talk.

Pausing a moment, Nick Thornton's image settled over her. He lived on the large island across the stretch of water. The distant homes looked lovely, large rambling houses with large boathouses, many two stories with rooms for guests. This kind of life she'd never experienced and never would.

She grasped her shoulder bag and crossed the street, heading toward the white building near the water, the marina's office, where people could gather information and perhaps book a fishing trip. Beyond the office, a white gazebo stood in a small patch of grass closer to the water, too small for a bandstand, but it added charm to the landscape.

Lake water and fish scented the air, a vital smell that made her feel alive. Rona leaned against the gazebo and drew in a deep breath as she regrouped her courage and reminded herself why she came to this town in a little hook of land in the upper peninsula.

Wondering what life might be like across the rolling blue water, she turned back and headed for her small sedan, but before she opened her car door, she noticed a grocery store across from the Harbor Inn. Her cabin didn't have a kitchen, but she could use some cereal and she could store milk in her cooler until she found something more permanent.

She veered across the street and headed inside. She gazed around the store sizing up what they had to offer. Cereal and milk for breakfast, a bag of chips and a six-pack of orange pop would serve her for now. She'd had a good meal at the inn and tomorrow she'd make more definite plans.

Rona paid the clerk, then stepped outside. Pressing the remote, she heard the comforting click of the locks. She shoved the grocery bag inside, then gave the lake a final look.

Her heart jigged a moment when she saw a broad-shouldered man with wind-tossed hair drive past her. His bristled jaw and solid features assured her. Nick. Rona followed his SUV with her eyes. When the road ended at the harbor, he turned left along the piers and boathouses.

Though feeling like a stalker, Rona climbed into her car and followed, curious as to where he was headed. Holding back, she saw him slow up and turn into a grassy area. She waited and soon he strutted from behind the cabins and crossed the street.

She rolled forward, seeing him march along the pier and stop in front of a good-size speedboat.

Nick untied the front ropes, then stepped into the craft and removed the back moorings. He vanished inside the cabin, and in a moment, she heard the motor hum and saw the boat head into the lake.

Her curiosity growing, Rona rolled closer to the pier and put her sedan in Park. She followed the wake of the bow as Nick headed to the big island. Nick steered along the shoreline, then rounded the bend. Marquette Island. It had to be.

She could picture his home, like him, manly and sturdy, but the image caused her to pause. He hadn't worn a ring but he could still be married. He had a son. She lowered her gaze, mortified that she'd been ogling a man who might very possibly have a wife.

Rona shifted into gear, turned around in the nearest driveway and headed back to Highway M-134, determined to keep her curiosity under control.

The motel appeared ahead. Hardly a place to call home, but she would make the best of it until she had the chance to find a rental she could afford. The job offer at Harbor Inn had been a gift from God.

God. She and God had been estranged for a long time. All her life she'd believed that the Lord guided her steps, but the day her brother duped her into giving him a ride had been the day she figured God might guide other people's plans but He'd allowed Satan to guide hers. Where had her fortress and shield been that day?

The remembrance shot through her and she didn't want any part of the recollection. Her life had nearly ended that day, and instead of struggling with it, she preferred to pretend it hadn't happened. That's why she'd moved away.

She pulled in front of her log cabin and dug into her bag for the key. Logs seemed to be the popular building material in the area. It made sense; Nick had mentioned his family were loggers and she realized logging still provided jobs for many workers. Too bad she wasn't a strong, outdoorswoman. Logging could provide her with a good income.

Nick had been on her mind since she'd met him. When he'd slid the newspaper in front of her, she decided at first it had been because he knew she wanted a better job than being a waitress, but when she saw the housekeeper ad, she wondered if he'd been interested in hiring her.

She questioned her good sense. The man didn't know her. She could be a thief or an addict…anything. Why would he consider her?

She couldn't imagine living in a house on an island, a big house with lovely furniture and at least some luxuries. Housekeeper? Could she handle a job like that. Why not? She'd cleaned many houses—her parents, her own when she'd been married, and then the variety of apartments she'd called home for short periods of time. Housekeeping as a job would hardly pay better than the waitress job. Still, it offered a room. Wondering why she'd let her mind wander to the ridiculous, she stopped herself from second-guessing.

A long, lonely evening lay ahead of her when she stepped inside the single square bedroom with a small bathroom. One glaring overhead bulb hung from the ceiling and a single lamp sat on the nightstand where she placed her purse and room key. She pulled open the brown-and-green plaid curtains to let in the five o'clock light. Night still came early in the north and she longed for long summer evenings.

She tossed the potato chips on the dresser along with the box of cereal, then checked her cooler for ice. Low. She'd need to add some cubes from the motel's stash until she could buy a bag.

Sinking into the only easy chair, Rona looked around the room with its dark walls, mass-produced paintings and thread-worn towels beside the sink. What would it be like to live in one of those lovely homes on Marquette Island or any island for that matter?

She twiddled her thumbs, wishing she'd picked up a magazine and the newspaper. She needed to find a place to live. The TV remote lay on the nightstand. She pointed it at the TV. Snowlike fuzz dotted the screen. She pressed another button and a news program brightened the room. The newscasters appeared to have orange-colored skin.

Forcing herself to watch, she sank back into the chair, but the distorted colors and unfamiliar names and places left her feeling even more alone.

Why had she come here? She could have lost herself in a big city somewhere else. She'd had reasons to run away. They made sense to her, but making the move had been harder than she realized. At home she had a couple of friends and a father who'd spent most of his lifetime drunk. It hardly seemed worth sticking around the Detroit area and dealing with her brother again for them. Her brother had hurt her—disappointed her—too many times.

Yet she loved him. They were kin and she knew that should mean something. To him, it meant someone to rip off and manipulate. At least being home meant memories of her mother and the familiar, as bad as it had been sometimes.

She snapped the off button and picked up the ice bucket. Outside, she located the motel's ice supply, filled the container and returned to her room.

What would people who lived on the island be doing? She couldn't see the water from the highway motel, but she tried to imagine. Nick was probably sitting in front of the TV watching sports or the news while waiting for his wife to prepare dinner. She glanced at her watch. Maybe they'd eaten already. She pictured a cozy nook with a white tablecloth, the family chatting over dinner.

Maybe Nick wasn't married. He needed a housekeeper, so possibly he was single, raising a son alone. Did he cook dinner or live on frozen meals as she so often did?

Enough. She shot from the chair. She'd rather work the night shift at the restaurant than spend the evenings alone. She paced the room, looking outside at the occasional car that shot along the highway. Goaded by her boredom, Rona thought of Shirley Bailey and tried to remember where she lived. She couldn't just drop by without calling.

With a purpose in mind, Rona headed to the motel office. The woman she'd seen earlier greeted her as she entered.

Rona smiled and leaned against the counter. "Do you have a local telephone book I could use?"

"Certainly." The woman reached into a niche below the desk and brought up a scrawny book that caused Rona to grin.

"Thanks," she said, opening the cover. This time Rona couldn't control her quiet chuckle. The book covered not only Hessel, but Cedarville, Rockport and other small cities nearby. She located the Hessel section and scanned the B's. Bailey. Samuel Bailey. Shirley still used her husband's name in the directory. Rona had tried to forget her husband's name as soon as she could.

She dug into her purse for a pen and paper and jotted the number on the back of her grocery receipt. With thanks, she slid the book toward the woman and stepped outside.

Heading for her car, she pulled the cell phone from her shoulder bag, then leaned against the sedan and pressed in the Bailey phone number.

Nick stepped onto his dock and moored the boat. He looked up the incline to the house—the lonely house. Though he and Gary seemed like strangers, his son made noise and sometimes had breakfast or dinner with him. He wished he knew how to talk with Gary. They were like two islands connected by a drawbridge that had risen and never came down again.

He wondered if all parents of teenagers felt like he did. He barely knew Gary's friends anymore. He didn't bring them home and avoided talking about them, and the ones he knew from church had faded from Gary's life. Nick didn't even know the girl his son had wrapped in his arms at the school.

Facing that things had to change, Nick drew in a breath and headed inside. The pervading trees blocked the lowering sun except for the living room and the dining room. He snapped on a light to brighten the gloom that surrounded him.

The kitchen sink still held their cereal bowls from the morning. Nick rinsed them and slipped the bowls into the dishwasher. He drained coffee from the carafe, cleaned the used grounds and made a fresh pot. The silence pressed against his ears except for the soft groan of the water warming in the coffeemaker.

He sank onto a kitchen chair, his mind drifted to the sunny diner in Hessel and the intriguing woman he'd met. Nick had seen more sparkle in her eyes than he'd seen in years.

Yet beneath the glint of curiosity and humor, she'd been wary. He sensed it. But why wouldn't she be? He'd been a stranger who invited her to sit with him and then talked in circles.

Nick should have asked her if she'd consider a housekeeping job. He called it that, but he needed someone in the house for more than housekeeping. Nick longed for someone to bring life to his home as well as keep the dust bunnies from multiplying and taking over. Most of all he wanted someone to keep an eye on Gary.

His past housekeeper, Angie, had decided to move to a big city, as she'd called it. He chuckled. If she thought St. Ignace was a big city, wait until she laid her eyes on Bay City or Saginaw.

Rona, he guessed, had come from the city. Maybe even Detroit. She had that look about her, and he heard concern in her voice about finding work and getting settled in the small town. Hessel's population was even smaller than Cedarville where Gary's high school was located.

The thought reminded him of his difficulties with Gary. Cedarville, that was the problem. He knew people in Hessel, but not as many in Cedarville. He didn't have as many connections there. Maybe he could get involved in some way. The idea rattled in his head. He had so little time. How could he get involved?

The scent of coffee aroused his senses. He rose and filled his favorite cup, then ambled into the living room where he could look out at the lake. Shades of gold spread across the water; he watched the changing sky for a moment, then headed for the family room and caved into the recliner. He leaned his head against the cushion and looked through one of the windows beside the fireplace. The flowering trees and the darkening leaves reminded him that summer was almost here.

He looked away from the pleasant view as his mind headed toward his problems. What could he do to make a difference in his and Gary's lives? He couldn't go on like this. He had businesses to run, responsibilities to handle and now a son who appeared to hate him. He closed his eyes, hoping God would send him a message, anything to give him a hint of where he'd gone wrong.

When he opened his eyes, he saw her picture on the mantle. Jill. Her face laughing into the camera. He'd lived with the other side of Jill as well, the brooding side. Studying the photo he noticed Gary looked like her. He only had Nick's light brown hair and maybe a similar smile, the smile he hadn't seen much lately.

Nick rose and lifted the framed photograph. Each time he saw it, guilt knifed his heart. He slid it into the small secretary desk drawer. He didn't need to be reminded of what he'd done. Life had moved on and Jill was in heaven, happier than she could have ever been on earth. He knew that for sure.

The sun had faded and Nick snapped on the light and ambled to the kitchen. Too weary to make dinner, he tossed lunch meat on two pieces of bread, took a big bite and headed back to the recliner.

By the time he'd settled back and tilted the chair, the sandwich had vanished. With a final sip of coffee, Nick closed his eyes, mulling over possibilities. He had batted zero finding a housekeeper. He just needed to be direct and see if Rona would be interested. At least he'd have one thing off his mind if she accepted.

Rona shifted in the comfy chair, feeling good to be here again in the Bailey's cozy home.

"For a minute there, I didn't recognize your name when you called." The elderly woman grinned. "But then I remembered you were the little blond girl with straight hair and bangs."

Straight hair and bangs. Memories swept over Rona. "That was me." Her mind flew back to her skinny legs and scrawny body. She'd hated it then, but she looked at her rounder figure now and wished she had a little of that thinness today.

"You visited a few times with Janie, I remember."

A few times. Yes, and the trips had always been such a wonderful reprieve from her difficult childhood. The Bailey house brimmed with sunshine, smiles and a cozy comfort she'd never known at home. Her mother tried, but her father had dashed all attempts to the ground.

"At least that's what I recall," Mrs. Bailey said as if questioning her own recollections.

Rona swallowed her memories. "You're right, Mrs. Bailey. I visited numerous times. I haven't seen Janie in years. I hope she's well."

"She's fine. Lives in California with her husband and three children. Sweet kids."

Husband and three kids. California. "That's great." Envy prickled along Rona's neck, thinking of friends happily married with kids. Kids she'd never have.

"I'm so glad you called tonight. There's nothing good on TV on Mondays."

Rona held back a laugh. "I'm not sure any night is good, especially trying to watch anything on the motel's TV."

Mrs. Bailey leaned closer. "Where are you staying?"

"Up the road. Some small cabins."

She nodded.

Rona wondered if she had heard her. "Just up the road," she said, raising her volume.

"Those small cabins?"

"That's right." She'd wondered why sometimes the woman had given her a blank look. Now she knew.

"How long are you visiting?"

She'd told her earlier. Rona cranked up her volume. "I'm planning to stay for a while. Settle down here, I think."

Her eyes brightened. "Really?" She cocked her head as if thinking. "You'll have to drop by now and again. I don't have lots of visitors nowadays since Sam's gone."

"I was sorry to hear about his passing."

Greeted by another blank stare, Rona repeated herself, this time, louder.

"Yes, it's been a little over a year since Sam died." She looked across the room a moment and Rona followed her gaze but didn't see anything particular that had drawn her attention. "Hard to believe he's gone, except it's lonely."

Lonely. Rona knew that word well. "I'm sure it is. I'd be happy to stop by when I can."

Mrs. Bailey perked up. "Good. I'll make cookies."

Sadness swept over Rona. She'd felt lonely when her mother died, but she'd built up a wall to protect herself. But recently that protection had failed and the same hollow feeling seemed to overwhelm her again at times.

"Are you retired?" She leaned back, her mind seeming to drift.

Don't I wish. But when the question struck Rona,

she closed her jaw and wondered if she looked that old. "I'm too young to retire. I found—"

The elderly woman's eyes widened. "What was I thinking?" She shook her head. "I know you're a young woman. Sometimes my mouth doesn't check in with my brain."

This time Rona laughed out loud. "That's okay. Mine doesn't either. I found a job in Hessel this afternoon at the Harbor Inn." She told the woman what had happened.

"Doesn't the Lord provide when we need Him?"

The Lord? Rona figured it had been her quick decision and downright luck.

"Do you have friends here?"

Friends. Rona's shoulders lifted in a sigh. "Not really. I met another waitress today named Mandy, but she's rather young." Nick's image sprang to her mind. "And I talked with a man named Nick."

"Nick? The only Nick I know around here is Nick Thornton."

Rona's pulse tripped. "You know him?"

"Everyone knows Nick Thornton. He owns some big businesses around here. Even ran for city council before his wife died. Such a tragedy."

Relief washed over her, then backlashed and the sensation rocked her. What did she have to be relieved about?

"He's a good Christian man. If you get tired of working at Harbor Inn, you might ask him about a job. I'm sure he knows what's happening in town."

Her mind flew back to the restaurant. She could see Nick's deep scowl when he said there was work if you knew where to look. They'd become silent while she waited for him to say more, but he hadn't. "Where should I look?" she'd asked, and his answer had set her back. "At me."

At him? Had that been what he meant, only that he knew where there were jobs? She'd hoped he'd been referring to his housekeeper position. She eyed her watch. "I suppose I should get back to the motel before I can't find my way home in the dark."

"Too late." Mrs. Bailey swung her arm toward the window. "It's already dark. You're welcome to spend the night."

"Thanks, but I need to get back. Anyway, I've been in the dark before." Rona heard the unintentional irony of her statement.

She'd been in the dark too long, but not anymore. Never again.

Chapter Three

"Gary. You'll be late for school."

Nick listened and heard nothing.

"Gary!"

He stood at the bottom of the stairs, waiting. He didn't want to play the silent game with his son. That's what he'd received this past year. He'd tried everything to no avail and his frustration had grown to bitterness.

"Gary!" His voice boomed up the staircase.

No sound.

Gary hadn't awakened him last night when he arrived home. The recliner had been Nick's downfall. He'd fallen so sound asleep he hadn't heard Gary come in. When he woke, he'd checked his watch—midnight—turned off the TV and hurried upstairs to check on Gary.

When he peeked in his room, it was dark, but he'd seen Gary's bumpy form and felt relieved. He'd actually gotten home. Still he'd been tempted to wake Gary and find out what time he'd come in, but doing so would have been antagonistic. The situation had taught him a lesson. Nick realized he needed to stay awake if wanted to be a good father—his definition, not Gary's. To Gary a good father was one who doled out money, said yes to everything and never asked anything of him.

Nick gave another yell up the staircase, then shook his head, grabbed the banister and took the steps two at a time to the top. He charged down the hallway and blasted his fist against his son's bedroom door. "Gary!"

When he heard no sound, his pulse lurched. What was wrong? Tragedy happened in the blink of an eye. He'd experience it with Jill. The memory flooded him. God wouldn't let something happen to his son. *Please,* he whispered. He pushed the door open, his pulse throbbing in his temple.

In the muted light, Nick saw the tangled blankets and same lump. His pulse escalated and he felt weak.

"Gary." He stepped over shoes and clothing in clumps on the floor and grasped the blanket. He pulled it back. Empty. A pillow and twisted blankets created the form he'd seen. Intentional? He had no idea, but the possibility stabbed him and he prayed the lump had only been caused by Gary's usual messy treatment of his room.

Nick's stomach churned, but as he stepped back, he gathered his wits and strained to listen for the shower. Gary always took a shower in the morning. He darted to the bathroom farther down the hall. The door stood open. Struck by reality, Nick knew Gary hadn't come home last night.

He slammed his fist against the bathroom doorjamb. He felt as if he and Gary lived in two different worlds and nothing could unlock the door. At the same time, fear spiked his anger and his pulse kicked in again. A boating accident? Car accident?

Nick charged to the staircase and at the bottom of the stairs, he stopped and got a grip on himself. Yesterday Gary had mentioned Phil. Nick knew Phil. He even knew the boy's dad. He released a ragged breath, pulled up his shoulders and headed for the phone.

After finding the number in the phonebook, he punched it in, then waited as the telephone rang. No answer. His hope faded until he eyed his watch again. Phil's dad had probably left for work and his wife had perhaps driven the boys to school. When the answering machine clicked on, he started to hang up, then heard a hello.

"This is Gary Thornton's father. I—"

"The boys left for school already, Mr. Thornton."

"Then Gary did—" He stopped himself, ashamed to admit he hadn't known that his son had spent the night. "Thanks. I'll catch him later."

What kind of a father didn't know where his kid was? He gripped the receiver, wanting to throw it through the wall, then hung it up, knowing he was angry at himself as much as Gary.

Whose fault was their rotten relationship? Maybe his. He should ask for names and phone numbers of all his son's friends. He sank onto a kitchen stool and lowered his face in his hands. Lord, give me direction. Help me be the father I should be. I don't know what to say to Gary or what to do that won't bring a sneer.

Nick rubbed his face, his appetite gone though he'd

eaten little the night before. He pushed away the coffee he'd made, turned off the pot and headed outside. He'd have to deal with the situation the only way he knew how.

Walking down to the boathouse, Nick drew in the spring air, wishing he felt as filled with fresh expectation. Things were growing around him, but his life seemed to have died in a stagnant pool of regret. He could see shades of green burst from the trees after the starkness of winter and he longed to have his life fresh again. He yearned for hope of something new and shining in his life.

Instead, he faced an angry son and an empty bed. Jill had been gone for three years and though their marriage had its bad moments, Nick had prayed they would stick it out and bring their relationship back to life. Since her death his loneliness had never faded, the deep empty space in his heart filled with regret.

Turning the key, Nick heard the motor purr. He steered to the shoreline and docked in Hessel. He located his SUV behind Lindberg Cottages and as he pulled away, he let his attention settle on the Harbor Inn and on the pretty woman with the long, golden-streaked hair. Rona. A pretty name for a pretty lady.

He'd thought of her last night, sitting alone in the quiet house. Why had he been drawn to her? Maybe her generous offer to help Bernie had triggered his admiration. She'd captured his interest and it unsettled him. No woman had cut through his anguish until yesterday and Rona had done it without trying.

Heading for Cedarville and the school, Nick's mind darkened to his situation with Gary. Being a good business man, he wondered why he couldn't transfer the talent to raising a son. Each situation took control, planning and wisdom. He'd been trained in the business world. He knew it backward and forward, but he had no training to be a father.

Everything took training and talent. Rona had mentioned she'd been a waitress. She knew the job. That had been obvious.

As he watched her work, he saw she had spirit. He recalled Jill's lackadaisical approach to life. She wanted him to be more laid-back, but he'd been too honed to a structured work ethic. Now he realized he needed to change.

He had yesterday, sitting around Harbor Inn as if he had scads of time. Nick wondered what drove Rona. The look of concern in her eye when he'd first spoken to her had interested him, because it contrasted to her confidence as she worked.

The thought lingered as he pulled up in front of the school. He turned off the motor and headed inside to the front office. A secretary looked up from her computer. "Can I help you?"

"Attendance. Would you check to see if my son is in school?"

She rose and flagged him behind the counter. "Our attendance lady is down here. She might have the absence slips for this hour."

He followed her down the hall, then stood beside the desk and waited until the clerk looked up.

"And you are…?" the woman asked, her eyes questioning him.

"Gary Thornton's dad. I want to make sure he's in school today."

She nodded. "I saw him this morning." She turned to the computer, apparently typing in his name. "He's in history this hour." She shuffled through the pink slips and nodded. "He's not on the absence list, so he must be here. Do you want to speak with him?"

Nick struggled a moment for the answer. "If I could."

She wrote the room number on a slip of paper and handed it to him.

"Thanks," he said, clasping the paper and stepping through a door to the hallway. He glanced at the note and grinned. A hall pass. He hadn't seen one of those since he was in school. He headed to the end of the corridor. H Hall the metal placard said on the wall. Gary was in H109.

Nick eyed the numbers above the doorway. H105. H107. He faltered outside of H109. What now? He could see the teacher pacing in the front of the room through the glass slit in the door. A hum of voices came through the transom. He straightened his back and knocked.

The hum quieted, then raised in volume and he could hear the teacher's shushing. He watched her head his way and the door opened. She appeared to be surprised to see an adult.

"Can I help you?"

"I'm Gary's dad. Gary Thornton. Could I speak to him a minute."

"He's reviewing for a test, but he can have a minute."

The door surged closed and Nick felt his heartbeat kick. When the door sprang open again, Gary's scowl faced him.

"Dad!"

Nick waved to him to close the door, then motioned him to step away from the window. "Where were you last night?"

"Phil's. He couldn't get the car to bring me home."

"Why didn't you call?"

Gary's face twisted. "I'm not a child."

"As long as you live under my roof, you'll follow my rules, Gary."

"I can move out."

"No, you can't."

"Oh, so I'm bound to you like a slave."

Nick's stomach knotted and he saw he had headed into a direction he hadn't meant to go. "Gary, look. I don't want a slave and I don't want a prisoner. I want a son. I care about you. I was worried until I called Phil's."

Gary drew back. "You called Phil's?"

"Yes. His mother said you'd left for school."

"Great." Gary jammed his hands into his pockets. "I suppose you told her I hadn't gotten permission to stay."

Nick looked into his eyes. "No, I didn't. I didn't want to ruin the trust you have with Phil's parents."

Gary's gaze flickered, as if weighing what Nick had said. Trust. The whole mess was about trust. Nick wanted to trust his son and maybe that's what he needed. They both needed to earn each other's trust.

"We can talk later. You're taking a test. I'm glad you're in school and I'm glad you're safe. I lost your—" He shook his head, biting back his words. Nick had lost his wife, but how could he forget Gary had lost a mother. "I lost my temper."

Gary's face softened and he lowered his head.

"Go back inside. I'll see you at home."

Gary put his hand on the knob, then glanced over his shoulder as he stepped back into the classroom. "Thanks."

His single word had nearly been lost by the students' noise inside the classroom, but Nick heard it. He stood a moment in thought, then turned and strode outside, thanking God that he'd found words that had made a difference. He hadn't heard a thank-you from Gary in more than a year.

Nick climbed into the SUV, struggling with what to do about the situation. He could ground him until—until what? He promised to be a good boy? Until he promised to show respect. That would work for a beginning, but at the moment the thank-you had salved Nick's frustration and he let the question drop.

When he arrived at the marina, Nick started down toward his boat, but changed his mind and ambled toward the restaurant. Maybe he should eat a late breakfast, then get back to his paperwork.

Breakfast. Who was he kidding?

When he stepped inside, the aroma of coffee and bacon danced around him. He scanned the room. No Rona. Then the kitchen door swung open and she came out wheeling a cart into the dining room.

"Have a seat anywhere," Bernie called through the serving window.

Nick gave him a wave and noted the direction Rona had moved in to clear tables. He found a window spot along the front and watched her.

Rona stacked dishes, tossed silverware into a plastic container and piled the soiled dinnerware into the cart. She wiped off the table and spun around before she saw Nick.

Her face flickered from surprise to an uneasy smile. She raised her hand in a hello and continued to the next table. She placed a cup and spoon on the cart, swiped the table clean, and parked the cart beside the counter before approaching him with her order pad. "Hi." She gave him a questioning look. "Can I help you?"

He needed help, but he wasn't sure anyone could solve his problems except the Lord. "How about a coffee and toast."

She tilted her head and frowned. "That's not much for a lumberjack."

It took a minute for her comment to register, then he felt his tension ease. "Okay, then add some scrambled eggs with cheese."

"And a side order of bacon?" She tapped the eraser end of the pencil against the pad.

He remembered the aroma that first struck him when he entered; his stomach gave a hungry gnaw. "And bacon."

"Coming right up," she said, her face relaxing to an easy smile.

Realizing he'd forgotten to pick up the morning paper, Nick rose and headed toward the door, but before going outside to the box, he spotted an abandoned edition folded at the end of the counter with no one around. He motioned toward the paper. "Anyone own this?"

A woman sitting nearby shrugged. "Looks like it's yours."

When he returned to his table he noticed the steaming coffee cup already waiting. She was fast. His gaze drifted toward the kitchen door. He shouldn't have walked off so quickly.

Sometimes he yearned for friendly conversation—different from business talk or a casual "nice weather" to the postman. He longed for a conversation about meaningful things, life and faith, even disciplining children.

He'd notice Rona's ring finger absent of a wedding ring and his speculation launched again.

His food appeared in the serving window. He knew it was his because no one else seemed to be waiting for an order. In a moment, Rona came out front, balanced the dishes along her left arm and headed his way.

"Here you go." She set the eggs and bacon in front of him followed by a plate of toast. She scooted the jelly dish closer. "I'll be back with a warm-up." She stepped away, then stopped. "Anything else before I go on break?"

The sun came through the window and highlighted the strands of gold in her shiny hair that curled upward just below her shoulders. "Some company."

"Sure thing." She lifted her chin as if to nod, then stopped. "Did you say company?"

He patted the table across from him. "I need some advice."

A frown returned to her face. "From me?" She pressed the flat of her hand against her chest. "You're kidding."

"Not at all."

She turned away and returned to refresh his drink,

then left. She surprised him by her abruptness. He knew he'd been presumptuous, but he really wanted to talk. He felt drawn to her for some reason.

Nick looked out the window, heavenward. God knew he had needs. Maybe God had guided him to someone like Rona. Maybe she had wisdom to offer him.

Glancing back at the kitchen door, he wished he'd taken a different tack. He'd pushed a friendship too quickly. It wasn't like him at all. Nick had never flirted, not even a playful innuendo, while he'd been married and never since Jill died. But in the past two days he'd been doing something and he wasn't sure whether it had been flirting or not.

A whish of sound drew him back as Rona settled across from him with a cup of coffee and a muffin. She pulled a paper napkin from the holder, took a sip of coffee, then leaned back. "I'm the worst person in the world to give advice."

"Why?"

She dropped her gaze and tore off a hunk of her muffin.

He watched her consume the bite, lick her lips and sip the coffee before she focused on him.

"I've never given myself good advice, so I don't expect to have wisdom for anyone else." She lifted her eyebrows as if to punctuate what she'd said.

"Do you have kids?"

"No. I was married once, but never had a child. It was best."

Her comment piqued his interest, but he'd learned his lesson and kept his mouth closed before he scared her away. "I have a son."

"Gary."

His eyes widened until he recalled yesterday. "You remembered."

She nodded, lifting her mug.

"He's sixteen."

Her concerned look changed to a chuckle. "Then you're lost and so am I when it comes to advice. Sixteen is a bad age."

"I know. He didn't come home last night."

Her smile faded. "Did you call the police?"

"I located him. He's okay. He stayed with a friend." Nick startled himself telling his personal problems to a woman he didn't know. "I don't suppose you want to hear this."

"It's tough raising a kid alone."

She looked uneasy and he glanced down at his left hand wondering if she'd surmised he was single from the lack of a ring. Better yet, from his presumptuous behavior.

Rona fingered her cup, then tilted her head as if to give him the answer to his unspoken question. "I heard your wife died a couple years ago."

She'd heard from who? Bernie? His shoulders knotted. What had Bernie told her? "It was three years ago."

"Three. That's still not very long. My husband's been gone for ten."

"Ten." He studied her interesting face, her well-shaped mouth and compelling eyes. "You never remarried?"

She shook her head and looked away.

From her reaction, he decided he'd asked enough

about that subject, but his interest didn't falter. "Bernie told you about Jill?"

Rona inched her gaze toward him. Jill?

"My wife."

"No. It was Shirley Bailey."

Bailey? He shrugged.

"She lives on Island View Road. She's my childhood friend's grandmother. I dropped by last night to say hello." She gave him a halfhearted disconcerted look. "I hadn't seen her in years and wasn't even sure she'd remember me."

The last comment intrigued him, but he let it slide. "I don't think I know her."

Rona gave a half-smile. "She said everyone knows Nick Thornton." She bit off a hunk of muffin. "She told me about your wife's death."

He searched her face, wondering if that had been all the woman had said, because he didn't want to go there.

"It was very sudden." He grasped the handle of his coffee mug and took a sip, hoping the pause would allow the topic to fade away. "Are you renting a place?"

She wiped her mouth with a napkin. "Not yet." She evaded his gaze.

He swallowed his next question, knowing it was too soon to ask and definitely bad timing.

"I need to find a place to stay. Do you know anyone who has a flat around here? Shirley told me you knew what was happening in town." Her questioning expression turned him upside down.

Had she read about his job in the paper? If so, she'd certainly mention it. The image of his boathouse apart-

ment flashed in his eyes and he bit his tongue to control
the offer, sensing it was a bad idea. He'd already come
on too fast. "Not offhand, but I'll keep my ears open."

"Thanks. I'd appreciate that."

He fiddled with his paper napkin, hounded by the
desire to be honest about his job opening with room
and board, but if she said no, then he would wish he
had waited. She'd just started the job with Bernie and
he really didn't know her at all. He liked her, that was
true, but could she handle Gary? He wanted to do
what was best for his son. He'd be wise to give himself
time to know her better.

When Nick refocused, Rona eyed her watch.

"Time's up." She looked disappointed as she slipped
her mug onto the empty muffin plate. "I'd better get
back to work before Bernie fires me on my second
day."

Nick managed a grin, but had to fight from praying
for that exact thing to happen.

Rona settled into the easy chair, snapped on her
bedside lamp and pulled the newspaper from the table.
She needed to find a place to rent. This motel situation would drive her mad. The past four days these
cramped quarters had felt like a jail cell. The thought
prickled up her arms.

Jail. Prisoner. The words jarred her and she thought
of her brother. Would Don find her? He would be
paroled some time this month, and though he was her
brother, she wanted no part of him. He'd nearly ruined
her life.

She spread the newspaper on her lap, but before she

could focus, the alien jangle of her cell phone jarred her. The cell had been meant for emergencies. She hadn't given the number to her father, only a friend who promised to let her know if anything went wrong at home.

Rona closed the paper and dug into her bag. The irritating jingle continued as she gazed at the number without recognition. She said hello, and as soon as she heard the voice, she remembered. She'd given her number to Mrs. Bailey.

"I baked cookies today. Chocolate chip and peanut butter. I wanted to make sure I had something you'd like."

"I love them both, Mrs. Bailey," Rona said, hearing pleasure in the elderly woman's voice.

"Would you like to come over for a visit? I'd love your company."

Again? She'd only been there last night. She eyed the newspaper, feeling guilty, but knowing she didn't want to give the older woman false hope of being a constant companion. Though she was pushing forty, Rona wanted to live a little before ending her social life.

"I have some things to do tonight, but how about tomorrow?"

"Tomorrow?"

Rona heard disappointment in the woman's voice.

"All right, then." She paused as if grasping for another comment. "I'll make tea tomorrow."

"Tea sound wonderful, and I know the cookies will be as good tomorrow as today."

She heard hesitation in Mrs. Bailey's voice, but she must have accepted her excuse. "I'll be waiting," the woman said, her cheery voice zapping Rona with sadness as they said goodbye.

Rona fell back against the chair, wishing she didn't feel so guilty. That could be me one day, she thought. Lonely. Alone. Mrs. Bailey and she had that in common. Yet the older woman had enjoyed a full life with a husband she loved. Rona had life to look forward to if she could stop running and settle somewhere safe, somewhere she felt free.

Pulling herself from her reverie, Rona unfolded the small newspaper again and flipped through the pages until she found the rental ads. She read the few entries, disappointed. Most of them offered cabins by the month or week. The only other ad she saw wasn't what she wanted. She had no desire to rent a house. A flat or apartment would serve her purpose well.

She turned the paper over to the Help Wanted ads and scanned the page. She didn't see Nick's ad for a housekeeper. Why hadn't he asked her? She'd given him every opportunity. He'd probably found a woman already. The possibility weighted her shoulders. Living on an island would have been wonderful—a beautiful setting, room and board, and a paycheck. What more could she want?

And, best of all, Don would have a difficult time finding her, or at least getting to her. He loved to ride into her life like a knight with all kinds of promises and then leave her eating dust.

Dust. Rona licked her dry lips and realized she needed something to drink. She rose and reached for the cooler, pulled out an orange pop and nabbed the potato chip bag.

When she settled back, she picked up the newspaper again to read the local news. She wanted to become familiar with the town she'd chosen to live in. As she placed her thumb on the edge of the daily paper to turn the page, Nick's ad lay just below her finger. How had she missed it earlier? Her pulse rose as did her hopes. Maybe Nick thought she wouldn't be interested so he hadn't offered her the job. Rather than second-guessing, she could just apply and get it over with. If he said no, she would just have to deal with it.

Then reality smacked her between the eyes. Nick knew she wanted a better job. He knew she needed a place to stay, but he hadn't offered her the position. He could have asked. Nothing had stopped him, except his own choice.

Nick hadn't given her a thought.

Chapter Four

Nick closed his car door and stood outside waiting to hit the remote while Gary sulked inside the SUV. Last night Gary had mentioned he might get home late from school again today, and, certain that his son planned to get away with something else, Nick had met him at the end of the school day, and this time insisted he go home with him.

Yesterday, he'd tried to control his frustration and broached the subject about Gary's overnight stay at Phil's and set down some rules. Gary only shrugged and blew him off. Rather than fight, Nick decided to give the situation thought and prayer. Today, he hoped to move a mountain.

"You can play the silent game with me," Nick said when Gary finally dragged himself from the passenger seat, "but we really need to talk."

With a half glance, Gary slammed the door and strutted past him. "Talk."

"I have been. Now it's your turn."

Gary dug his hands into his pockets and kicked at

the tufts of broad-leaved grass as they headed toward the lake. The progress they'd made earlier that morning had faded.

Disappointed, Nick looked at the stretch of water and knew talking was impossible over the roar of the motor, anyway, he needed to focus on steering the boat, not dealing with Gary. He looked down the sidewalk toward Harbor Inn, drawn there by the need for dinner he didn't want to cook and at the thought of seeing Rona. This would give him a chance to introduce Rona to Gary.

He tilted his head toward the restaurant. "Let's catch dinner in town."

Gary stopped on the sidewalk without looking up.

"Aren't you hungry? I don't feel like cooking tonight." He motioned again toward the inn. "Harbor Inn has good food."

Gary lifted his shoulders in an I-don't-care attitude and followed.

Nick knew there was little purpose in talking to Gary when he was in a bad mood, but maybe in the quiet atmosphere he could steer the conversation toward something that would relieve the tension. He wished they had someplace neutral where they could relax and be father and son.

They walked in silence, and when they stepped through the door, the smell of corned beef filled the air. Nick drew in the scent as he passed the counter toward the tables. Gary settled into a chair before Nick could point out a table, so Nick sat, wishing they'd gotten closer to the window. Rona usually waited tables in that section.

The kitchen door opened and Mandy came out,

strutting across the floor and passing them each a menu. "Need a minute?"

Nick didn't open his, but eyed Gary as he perused the choices. "I'll take the corned beef dinner with black coffee."

She retrieved his menu and waited.

"Rib dinner and a beer."

Mandy gave Nick a questioning look, then laughed. "Root beer coming right up."

Gary looked toward the window, then snarled. "Great."

She collected his menu and left.

Nick managed to control his temper. "Why did you say that? To upset me?"

"What's wrong with a beer?"

"Besides being sixteen, we don't drink in this family."

"Mom did."

Nick's pulse skipped. "What are you talking about?"

"I saw her. She had a bottle of wine or something in the back of the cabinet."

Nick tensed as memories flooded his mind. "She used it for cooking." Did she? He wasn't sure, but it made sense.

"Right. That's what she told me, but I saw her drinking it."

Nick's hand trembled and he tucked it beneath the table. "You were young then, Gary. Maybe you didn't see right."

"I was almost thirteen, Dad. I wasn't blind."

Nick struggled to keep his composure. He'd suspected Jill had a drink once in a while before she died, but he never drank with her. He never brought liquor into the home. He believed drink could lead to sin and he didn't want any part of it.

Mandy appeared with their drinks and two bowls. "The dinners come with salad." She set one in front of each of them. "What kind of dressing?"

They gave her their preference and she walked away while Nick looked at Gary and decided to drop the subject of drinking for now. He needed to deal with it himself. Jill drinking. That could explain so many things.

"How'd you do on the test?"

Gary shrugged. "I don't know for sure. Okay, I guess."

"Good." The small talk would get them nowhere, but it might soften Gary into having a regular conversation. Mandy delivered their dressings, and Nick looked toward the kitchen, wondering if Rona was working today. He hadn't seen her and his letdown surprised him.

He'd missed her yesterday, too, spending the day on Drummond at his resort. This time of year he had so much to do to get ready for the tourist season, and when he arrived back to Hessel, all he could think of was his problems with Gary and, though he'd intended to, he'd forgotten to stop in at Harbor Inn.

Nick nibbled on his salad while Gary poked at his. Pans and dishes rattled in the kitchen as their silence lengthened. He pushed the salad bowl away, trying to think of something to talk about that wouldn't start an argument.

"Here you go." Mandy set their plates on the table, removed the salad bowls and said she'd return with refills.

Nick sliced off a piece of the beef. The rich flavor struck his taste buds, but his appetite had waned with his attempt to talk. He forked some cabbage and slipped it into his mouth, watching Gary hold a rib between his fingers and gnaw on the tender meat.

Mandy's shadow above him caught his attention and he lowered his fork. "No helper today?"

She frowned for a moment and then chuckled. "You mean Rona?"

Nick felt heat building at the nape of his neck. He nodded and grasped his fork.

"She worked the breakfast and lunch shift today and got off early." She glanced at Gary, then back at Nick. "You like her?"

The heat curved around the back of his neck and climbed. "I don't really know her."

Mandy eyed him, a question on her face.

"I was here the day she offered to pinch hit for Bernie. She just caught my attention."

"Right," Mandy said, giving him a wink. She spun around and headed back to the counter.

Nick focused on his meal, hoping Gary hadn't tuned in to the conversation, but when he looked up, he realized he had.

"Checkin' out the chicks, Dad?" A coy grin spread across his face.

Nick gave him the toss of his hand. "Eat your ribs and wipe the barbecue sauce off your cheek."

Gary picked up a napkin and dragged it across his face, but his expression hadn't changed and Nick felt like a kid caught with his hand in his dad's wallet.

Heading for Mrs. Bailey's, Rona watched the sun sink in the sky like her sinking spirits when she thought about the difficulties she still had to face. But the sun always rose again and perhaps she had to learn from it. Night might fall, but the light could overcome the darkness. She remembered similar verses in the Bible, verses of encouragement and hope.

The greatest hope she experienced lately had been to move away from the Detroit area to start a better life somewhere else, but that depended on her and her attitude. She could talk her way into the pits or she could look for the sunshine she knew could be there.

Yesterday, she'd been disappointed. Though Nick had come into Harbor Inn the day after she'd first met him—in fact, he'd come twice—yesterday he hadn't come at all. She'd spent the day craning her neck, looking at the door.

She shouldn't care since she'd talked herself into snubbing him if he showed up. It was a bite-your-nose-to-spite-your-face situation that her mother always talked about. But Rona figured if Nick didn't think she was worthy of his housekeeping job, then why should she bother with him? While her reason told her one thing, her emotion told her something else.

Rona pulled into Mrs. Bailey's driveway and climbed from the car, feeling as if she'd made a mistake. She couldn't spend her days entertaining the elderly woman or having the woman entertain her. She needed to make friends of her own and find a life, but where and how? The questions tangled in her mind like seaweed.

The front door opened, and when she stepped inside, the scent of cookies filled the air. "Come into the living room," Mrs. Bailey said, motioning her ahead. "I have everything set up for us."

Rona flinched, knowing she'd disappointed the woman last night, but Mrs. Bailey beckoned her through the archway and she stepped into the living room, greeted by a teapot covered with a cozy and a plate of cookies. Napkins and condiments nestled on the tray as if the elderly woman had given much thought to presentation.

"Thanks, Mrs. Bailey. I—"

"Please, call me Shirley. I miss hearing my name. Sam sometimes called me Shirl, but Shirley will sound so good."

Rona's chest tightened at the look in the woman's eyes. "I'd be happy to, Shirley." She gave the woman a tender grin.

Shirley's eyes sparkled. "You could have cookies like this everyday, you know, if—"

Fearing what was coming next, she patted the outside of her hip. "I have to watch my weight."

Shirley shook her head. "You look gaunt to me. You need some good home-cooking, and so I was thinking…"

The cookie lodged in Rona's throat.

"I have plenty of room here and I'd love you to share my home with me. I would enjoy the company."

Rona couldn't respond. The offer, though sweet, sounded dire to her. She could easily sit in a rocker and watch her life pass her by, but that was not the life she wanted.

Shirley studied her, her face expectant, and Rona struggled to answer. She grasped for a solid reason why she couldn't stay. "That's a lovely offer, but I'm not sure it's a good idea." She grasped for a logical reason. "My plans are still up in the air." It's all she could think of that fast.

"I thought you were staying in Hessel."

She pushed herself into a corner. "I am, but I—I." I what? The words lodged in her throat. "I noticed an ad for a housekeeper job and the offer includes room and board."

"Really? Where is that?"

Rona hesitated, wanting so much to back up and rethink what she'd said. "It's nothing, really. I haven't applied." She waved her words away.

"Tell me. I'll advise you."

Shirley's eager face melted her resistance. "Nick Thornton needs a housekeeper. I saw it in the news-paper."

"Nick Thornton."

Rona had never heard Shirley's voice rise with such enthusiasm.

"That would be wonderful. He's a kind man and you just never know."

Rona drew back, thrown by her last comment. "Never know what?"

"What the good Lord has in store."

A frown pulled at Rona's forehead. "What do you mean?"

"God guides our steps. You never know what His plan is for you."

Rona wanted to rebut the statement, but she could see that Shirley's faith was strong and she decided she wasn't armed enough to dispute what she said. "The Lord and I bump heads quite often, Shirley."

"Then you're not listening to Him. You know we're

Jesus's lambs, and He's our shepherd. He holds us in His arms and carries us close to His heart. We can't butt heads when we're against His bosom."

That was her problem. Rona hadn't been close to Jesus's bosom in the past couple of years. She'd struck out on her own, thinking she could handle her own life and trials.

Shirley looked expectant and Rona didn't know what to say.

"Lambs are known for being dumb, Shirley. I think I'm one of them."

Shirley laughed. "No you're not. Maybe you've just strayed off, but He'll find you. Never fear." She retrieved her cup again and took a sip, a thoughtful look on her face. "I imagine Mr. Thornton is lonely on that island, raising a son on his own. It's not easy."

"I don't suppose it is."

"He could use a nice young woman to give him a hand. You should take the job."

Rona hesitated. "He hasn't offered it yet."

Shirley's eyes twinkled. "But he will."

"I wouldn't be so sure. But if he offers, I'll accept."

"I know you will, dear. That boy needs a mother."

Mother? Rona drew back. "I meant the offer of housekeeper, Mrs….Shirley. Nothing more."

Her chuckle filled the air. "Let the Lord take care of that, Rona."

Rona nearly choked. She grasped the tea and took a drink to calm herself. Mother. Wife. The words hung in her mind like the moon. She feared that's what Shirley meant earlier. Now she knew. "What happened to Nick…Mr. Thornton's wife?"

"She died."

"I know, but how?"

"It was tragic." She shook her head and appeared to end the conversation.

"Tragic?"

"A waterskiing accident. Mr. Thornton was behind the wheel."

The news hit Rona in the belly.

"And the boy was in the boat, too. He saw the whole thing."

Gary had seen his mother die? The news twisted around her heart. "Did she drown?"

"No, she ran into a wooden raft in the lake. Died almost immediately." She shook her head. "Such a sad thing for a boy to see."

Rona absorbed the news, her sorrow rising for Nick and his son. That kind of situation made her question the Lord. Why did he let those things happen? How could she trust a God who allowed terrible accidents to happen to good people?

The warm sun spread across the inn tabletops. Rona stretched her legs and arched her back against the chair, glad that the Saturday lunch crowd had slowed and she had time for a break. She noticed more activity in the marina the past few days. Memorial Day was next week and that meant tourists. Bernie told her to wear her running shoes to work.

She grinned, so pleased that she'd stumbled on the waitressing job and met Bernie. So far he'd been a kind boss and had told her the truth. Tips were excellent if she did her job well.

Out the window, Rona watched the Dream Sealer heading toward the pier, bringing back a boatload of fishermen. She longed to be out there with the wind and sunlight. Maybe one day she would splurge on a trip to see some of the islands that made up the Les Cheneaux area.

She hadn't seen Nick since Wednesday. Her plan to snub him had faded like the morning dew. The more she looked across the lake at Marquette Island, the more she wanted that job. Pride kept her from calling him. So did Bernie. She hated to let him down.

But Bernie had hired another waitress for the tourist crowd, and she was good. And with school letting out in a few days, he would have his pick of high school students eager to earn some college money for the summer. She salved her guilt by reminding herself that she'd been clear that if something better came along she'd take it.

The certainty that Nick had found a housekeeper swept over Rona like a wave in a storm. He was bound to have found someone by now, which meant she needed to find another place to stay, then maybe a new job. She'd gotten a discount at the motel for staying a week, but her week was up and she'd procrastinated in hopes—

Hopes. When did she count on her hopes working out?

"You look thoughtful."

Rona looked up and watched Mandy slide into the chair across from her.

"Wishing I were outside…and in my own place. I need to find a rental."

"Want help looking? I know of a studio apartment and I work the late shift tomorrow night. I have the morning."

She looked at the younger woman whose warm smile always made her feel liked. "I'd love it."

"So tomorrow, then? You're off, right? And Monday is a holiday."

"Bernie said we're closed on Monday. I'm surprised." Holidays meant tourists.

"He gives us Memorial Day because from then on, we're open. No rest for the wicked, as they say."

"So that's it." Rona nodded, understanding Bernie's motivation. "The other thing I really want to know is what to do around here for fun."

"Once you get to know the area, you'll be surprised at all the events going on—quilt shows, the antique boat show, River Rampage, even an Indian powwow. And just wait until the Fourth of July."

Rona grinned at her enthusiasm. "There's the problem. I don't know the area."

Mandy cupped her chin in her hand. "Okay. If you want to have some fun, we could do a little of that tomorrow, too."

"I'd love it."

Out of the corner of her eye, Rona saw a man's form approaching, her heart skipped to her throat, then sank. It wasn't Nick. She'd hoped, because the longer she waited the more she wished that he'd offer her the housekeeping job.

Mandy turned her head to follow her gaze, then looked back. "Waiting for someone?"

Rona shook her head.

Mandy let her question drop. "Ever been to Drummond Island?"

"No. I've never been anywhere but Hessel and Cedarville."

"Why don't you come to church with me in the morning, and then we can take the ferry to the island. We'll have lunch there. I know a great restaurant. It'll be fun."

Church? The vision billowed over Mandy's conversation. Rona shrunk beneath her offer. "How about getting together after church?"

Mandy shrugged. "Sure, and maybe we could check out the studio I mentioned."

"It's a date."

Mandy slid from the chair. "I'd better get back. I'm not on break like you are." She grinned and vanished.

It's a date. That's something Rona hadn't had in a long time with anyone. She looked out the window, drawn by the view and the sunshine. An SUV passed the inn, and her pulse quickened. Nick. She craned her neck to follow the vehicle until it turned the corner and headed toward the pier. Maybe he'd walk back and have dinner.

With her gaze riveted to the road, Rona waited until too much time had passed and her hope sank.

She lowered her head, disappointed in herself. She'd allowed fanciful thoughts to puncture reality. She'd lived in the real world long enough to know that dreams didn't come true.

Still she wished they did.

Chapter Five

Nick sat in his SUV on the Drummond Island ferry and gazed through the window at the limestone quarry with its powdery white trail leading away from the shore to Humps Road. He shifted in the seat and rested his head against the neck support.

After church, Gary had asked to spend the day with Amy's family. Amy, he'd learned, was the girl who'd been glued to Gary's side; Nick spoke to the girl's mother—with Gary's approval, to his surprise—and learned Amy's family had planned a picnic.

Another surprise had been Gary's agreement to attend worship without an argument, and though Nick knew he should be pleased, Gary's cooperation set him on edge. After the phone call to Amy's parents, Nick relaxed and, with the day free, he'd decided to put some time into his work at the resort.

He drew in a breath, sorry for so many things. He'd tried to be a good father after Jill's shocking death. Jill. The picture flashed through his mind of that horrible day, and like everyone who watched a tragedy happen, he replayed it in his mind, wondering what he could have done to make a difference and what had really happened. He was at a loss.

Gary's words had stabbed him since Friday. He wanted to grill him about Jill's drinking, but Gary had only been a boy and Nick shot the questions at himself. Gary may have been confused, and if not, then why hadn't Nick noticed? Or had he? He recalled smelling something like mouthwash on Jill's breath when he arrived home…late so often. Running two businesses had stolen time from his family.

He'd told himself Jill had freshened up for him, but now that he thought back, had it been alcohol he smelled? Jill's personality had changed, too. She'd stopped smiling when they were alone. Her cheery face only lit up in social settings. He figured she'd gotten tired of his long work hours, but he did it for her and Gary. He wanted them to have a good life. Jill liked nice clothes and jewelry. She liked—

He had no idea what she had liked. Gifts, jewelry, a new boat, a home on Marquette, he'd done it all for her and nothing had seemed to make her content.

He couldn't let go of the drinking issue. He and Jill never drank. At least, that's what he'd thought. Though he knew some Christians who saw no harm in a glass of wine, he'd always stayed away from it. But Jill? His head swam, struck with the possibility.

The ferry bumped the pier and Nick straightened in the seat and readied the SUV to roll across the ramp to the shore. He craned his neck to look in the back to make sure he'd remembered to put the box into the car.

He needed to stop at the Information Center with his new brochures. The way his mind had been he'd begun to question himself.

Pulling his mind from Jill and his flagging memory, he replaced it with his mission. He headed up Channel Road, and as he passed the Island Restaurant and Bakery, he remembered he wanted to stop on the way home for one of their great chocolate cakes. Maybe that would cheer up Gary.

He sped past and headed for Four Corners, the business center of the island and on the way to his resort. When he arrived at Warner's Cove Road, Nick pulled in front of the Information Center. He climbed out, lifted the hatch and pulled out the carton, then strode to the building.

When he swung open the door, Nick stopped cold and did a double take. The women's mouths dropped open as far as his had probably fallen.

Mandy's surprise turned to a smile. "Hi, Nick." She gave Rona a poke with her elbow as if to wake her from a trance.

"Hi," Rona said, her gaze shifting from him to Mandy.

Nick managed to harness his amazement "What are you two doing here?"

"Sightseeing," Mandy said.

He glanced in Rona's direction, but she didn't say a word.

Mandy tilted her head. "What brings you here?"

"Dropping off some resort brochures, then doing some catch-up at the resort. You know how it is getting ready for the tourists. They come in droves starting next week." He heard himself prattle on and stopped.

The two women just looked at him.

He shifted his gaze from Mandy to Rona, hoping she'd say something more than hi. "What have you seen so far?"

"Nothing yet," Rona said. "Just the ferry ride over and now we're here." She motioned to the wall of brochures.

"I brought her right to Four Corners. We're going to check out the shops." Mandy had clipped off the last of Rona's sentence. "But I have to be back for work so it's a short day. Before we left Hessel, I took Rona to look at a place to rent."

Nick kept his focus on Rona as his heart sank. *Look at a place.* "Did you rent it?" His direct question forced her to answer.

She shook her head. "I'm giving it thought."

He needed to talk with her privately. He grasped for a way. Then one struck him. He focused on Mandy. "I'd love you to stop by the resort. It's on Tourist Road. Do you know where that is?"

Mandy jumped in. "We have a map, but—" She looked at Rona. "I could drop you off, but I can't stay."

Rona frowned and bit the corner of her lip as if she wanted to say no. Finally she looked at him. "Thanks anyway. Maybe another time."

"I don't mind," Mandy said, appearing to hide a grin, then turned her attention to Nick. "You'll give Rona a ride home?"

"Sure will," he said, hoping he'd learn to control his skipping pulse.

Rona's shoulder lifted in a hesitant shrug. "I suppose it's okay if you don't mind, Mandy."

Mandy shook her head. "I wish I could stay. I'd love to see your resort."

Nick gave thanks that she couldn't, but he stood a moment, his previous plans dashing against his head. He'd decided to get to know Rona better before asking her about his job. He thought it best that she and Gary meet to see how they related. What had he been thinking by deciding to ask her to take the job without making sure it would work?

"We'd better get moving then," Mandy said. She motioned to the door. "Ready?"

Rona gathered the brochures and stuffed them in her shoulder bag. "I'll see you later, I guess."

"It's Maxton Beach Resort," Nick said, his voice sounding strained in his ears. "You can't miss it."

She turned away and he watched them head through the door. He stood there holding the heavy box of brochures and looked heavenward. *Lord is this Your doing? This meeting is too coincidental. It must be—* What? He couldn't find the words.

Rona could barely concentrate as they wandered through Suns' Dragoons and The Islander Shoppe. She'd picked up a knit top and eyed a novel, but passed on it. When they stepped outside, Mandy checked her watch and suggested they visit the Maxton Plains near Nick's resort.

"What's the Maxton Plains?"

"Hard to describe. It's an alvar region and considered a treasure because there are so few places like this on the earth. You'll have to see it."

"Let's go." Rona motioned toward the car, not

wanting to ruin their sightseeing, but anxious to get to the resort. Since she'd seen Nick, she'd felt topsy-turvy, totally upside down and sideways. The sensation made no sense.

Mandy pulled onto a grassy path and they bumped along to a parking spot. Rona looked out on a rocky field with tall grasses and pines in the distance, wondering what was the big deal. She stepped outside, noting the lichen and moss clinging to the rocks as barren as her life seemed.

Yet as they strode down the stony path, she noticed tiny wildflowers bobbing in the breeze—little blue harebells, clusters of flowers tucked among the rocks, including ones that looked like tiny yellow coreopsis. The plain had an earthy charm and maybe her rough life had a hidden charm, too. She just needed to find it.

Mandy gestured toward the expanse. "This is said to be four-hundred-and-fifty million years old, caused by glaciers and limestone bedrock."

Despite her antsy mood, the age impressed Rona, but when Mandy suggested leaving, she was happy to get to the resort.

On the way, Mandy talked, but Rona gave one word responses as her anxiety rose. In her eagerness to spend time with Nick, she hadn't thought about what she and Nick would talk about over the next couple of hours. She'd chatted with him at the diner, but she barely knew the man.

Still, if the conversation drifted to family, Rona knew she didn't want to talk about hers. Her difficult life didn't make good casual conversation. It seemed more appropriate for a psychiatrist's couch.

The sign rose in front of them and Rona viewed the massive white building with dark shutters sitting close to the water, then noticed the small cabins nestled in a pine woods.

Mandy pulled down the drive and stopped. "I'll drop you here. I imagine the entrance is over there." She pointed to the right.

"I'll find my way. Thanks so much." She grabbed the doorhandle and hesitated. "I hate to send you on the ride home by yourself."

"I'm a big girl. I've driven this many times before." She brushed her away. "Have fun. I'll see you later."

Rona stepped back and waved as Mandy backed out of the driveway and onto the road. She turned toward the hotel, realizing once again Nick's lifestyle and hers were so different.

"Over here."

Nick's voice came from a doorway toward the back of the building. Her heart skipped when she saw him. He looked so good to her with his amazing smile, and once again his hair looked ruffled by the wind. He beckoned, and she headed toward him, her nerves jumping.

"Glad you found the place."

She looked at him and noticed his jaw was prickled with a five-o'clock shadow. It added character to his already rugged look. Her hand twitched to touch his cheek with the winking smile lines. "I hope I haven't kept you. We stopped at the Maxton Plains."

"Great place. Not many areas like that on the earth. Did you know it's millions of years old?" He pushed open the door.

"Mandy told me," she said as she stepped inside.

She paused a moment and let her gaze sweep the large office—a wide desk, file cabinets, a computer, a table piled with brochures and more boxes on the floor.

"Sorry about the mess. We're late getting the mailing out. We send brochures to old customers and names we pick up from the tourist office. I want to drop a box of the brochures in Cedarville at the chamber of commerce." He pulled a file folder from a chair and motioned to her. "Have a seat."

She motioned to the pamphlets. "Can I help?"

He grinned. "I'm finished for today, but thanks anyway. Would you like a pop?"

"No, thanks, but I'd like to see the resort."

Pleasure filled his face. "Follow me."

He led her through another door that exited beside the registration desk. The lobby, a blend of stone and wood, featured a broad window that looked out to the bay. A few easy chairs and sofas were scattered into seating arrangements and through the window she could see a patio with natural-toned wicker furniture beneath a canopy roof. "Very pretty."

"Thanks." He headed toward a door on the right. "I'll show you one of our rooms."

She followed him into a corridor, then stepped inside a guest room. Soft coral-hued walls and a moss-green carpet greeted her. Draperies and a bedspread picked up the colors.

Nick crossed to the curtains and pulled them open. Behind was a wide window and a door that opened to a private patio that held a small wicker umbrella table and two chairs upholstered in the same cheery coral and green. "It's beautiful, Nick."

"We bring in fresh flowers every day and chocolates. Pretty fancy, huh?"

She chuckled at his pantomime putting the chocolate on a pillow. It seemed paradoxical with his outdoors look.

"The rooms are pretty much the same except for the cabins. We've gone more rustic there and we deliver breakfast in a basket."

"I wish someone would do that for me." When the words left her, she wished she hadn't said them. They sounded like a come-on and she'd already wondered what kind of woman he thought she was. He'd given her so much unexpected attention.

"Maybe someone will someday." He turned away and drew the drapes again, shutting out the light.

He grasped her arm and led her back into the lobby, then to his office. "I have a house on the island, too. It's not far from here." He gave her arm a squeeze when he released it.

Warning buzzers sizzled in her head. "This is enough for one day, but thanks." She felt breathless and when she looked at him, she realized he'd been taken aback.

"I wasn't suggesting anything, Rona. I'm sorry if it sounded like that."

She shook her head. "Don't be sorry." She wanted to tell him it was her jangled nerves, but she let it drop and so did he.

He dug his hand into a pocket and pulled out a ring of keys. "Let's get going."

Outside, he locked the office door and they settled into his SUV. When he pulled away, Rona looked down toward the water and the wide stretch of beach.

She struggled to find something to talk about. Instead, she settled into silence.

Nick turned on the radio and switched stations until he found music, then lowered the volume. He glanced at Rona and smiled. She tried to smile back, but her discomfort unsettled her. It wasn't fear that bothered her, it was that hopeful desire to be Nick's friend and to feel at ease in his company.

"What kind of rental did you find?"

His voice cut through the music and surprised her. "It's more of a studio apartment in a house. The price is good, but I'll feel as cramped as I do in the motel."

Quiet hung over them again, except for the country music drifting from the speakers. Nick looked ahead as a frown settled on his face, and he reached for the volume control and lowered the song to a faint hum. "I know a place that might work."

She faced him. "A place to live?"

He nodded.

"Really?" Her heart skipped, hoping it was what she wanted.

"You can move to the island with us."

Yes. That's what she so longed to hear.

He twisted for a second to face her. "It's not what you might be thinking, Rona. I know I upset you before."

She shook her head. "I understand."

"It's a job. I'm looking for a housekeeper and I have living quarters above the boathouse."

Above a boathouse. She'd heard about the guest-rooms. "I—I thought by now you'd filled the job. I read about it in the paper."

His eyes widened. "You didn't ask me about it?"

"No, I figured if you were interested you'd ask me."

He shook his head. "We both second-guessed each other."

Mixed emotion fluttered in her chest. He had been thinking of her.

She wanted the job so badly, yet she worried. She didn't know Nick well. And his son? How would she get along with him? Dealing with a teen could be frustrating. "I'd have to give Bernie notice if I take the job."

"Here's a thought. Come to the island tomorrow. I know Bernie closes on Memorial Day. You can check out the apartment and meet Gary. What do you say? I'll pick you up at the marina."

His look seemed so sincere that Rona couldn't have said no if she'd wanted to, but she didn't want to. "That sounds great and I'll have time to think about your offer." Think? That's all she'd thought about.

"I'm glad. We'll talk business tomorrow then."

She agreed, but her heart didn't want to talk business. Nick had wiggled into her life and she wanted to know him better. She wanted to talk about life and dreams. She wanted to talk about everything but the past. She had no desire to go there.

After Nick dropped Rona at her apartment, he stopped at the market to pick up steaks and groceries for a barbecue tomorrow, and after storing those away at home, he dashed into the guesthouse apartment and eyed the space.

He could picture Rona here with the sunlight streaming through the living room window and streaking through her honey-colored hair. Without a house-keeper, the apartment had been neglected. The room needed dusting and the carpet vacuuming. He headed into the bedroom. Though neat, it needed dusting, too. He checked the bathroom. The mirror gleamed, and he was grateful Rose had left the place in good condition. She'd had a good work ethic.

Sometimes he wondered why she'd really left. Had it been because of the tension with Gary? Nick knew his son could chase away an angel, but he prayed things would change. If he could keep calm and be the father Gary needed, he could move mountains with God's help.

Standing here will get me nowhere, Nick thought. He headed for the storage closet and pulled out items he needed for dusting and the vacuum. Moving around the room, he sprayed then swept away the dust, admiring the shine and wishing he could sweep away his problems as easily. Outside the sun had lowered in the sky and a palate of purple and coral spread across the horizon.

Beneath him, he heard the powerboat land at the pier. Gary had arrived home. He checked his watch. He'd come home on time. Nick dragged in a grateful breath. God was good.

Looking out the window, he saw Gary head toward the house. Nick strode to the doorway and stepped onto the landing. When Gary rounded the boathouse, Nick gave a call and beckoned to him.

Gary stopped and gave him a surprised look as he moved toward the staircase to the apartment. "What are you doing up there?" He ascended the steps.

"Dusting," he said, waving the cloth at him. "I've found a housekeeper, I hope, and I've invited the woman over tomorrow to take a look."

"Tomorrow? It's Memorial Day." His forehead knitted.

"I know, but it worked for her. Would you like to invite Phil over for steaks, or—" his preference came out next "—how about Amy?" Somehow he wanted to get to know this girl. Gary had always been stand-offish about his friends. "It would make the lady more relaxed I'm sure with other people here."

"It's a job, Dad. You don't have to entertain her."

Nick grasped for something sensible to say rather than what was in his heart. "I do need to show her the house. She'd have to live here."

"Why?"

"Just like Rose. She's new in town and has no other home in town, so it makes sense."

"But you don't know her, Dad. What's she like?"

"You'll see tomorrow when you meet her. She's been working at Harbor Inn for a few days."

A toying grin spread across his face. "Is this the chick you were looking for the night we had dinner there?"

"I wasn't looking for anyone." Heat rose on the back of his neck.

Nick watched Gary's expression as he processed what he'd said, and Nick could tell he still questioned him.

"What do you say? You want to call Phil? Amy?"

"I'll check with Amy. Her folks have another party so that's why they had a barbecue today." He took a step backward down the stairs but stopped. "You don't expect us to stick around the whole time, do you? Some of our friends are getting together."

"No, just come for dinner and meet Rona. Tell Amy we'll pick her up at the marina around noon."

He shrugged. "Okay." He swung around, then turned back. "Rona, huh?" He winked, then bounded down the steps and up the hill to the house while Nick watched him, knowing he'd have to watch himself tomorrow.

He tossed the dust-cloth into the air and caught it before stepping inside. One job done. Two, really. He'd dusted and talked with Gary. Once he vacuumed he'd go inside and plan their meal.

He wanted things to be perfect for Rona.

Rona. He closed his eyes and prayed that what he felt in his heart was God's leading and not his own longing.

Chapter Six

Rona stood near her car and watched the speedboat head for the pier. As it neared, she could see Nick at the helm and another young man seated beside him. Gary, she assumed. The only other person on the pier was a teenaged girl sitting on the wooden planks and swinging her feet back and forth as if waiting for someone, too.

As the boat nosed to the wharf, Rona left her car and headed to the pier. As she stepped onto the wide planking, the girl rose in pink Capri pants so tight Rona wondered if they were painted on and strode toward the boat.

Gary tied the rope, then waved to the girl and hurried forward as Nick sent Rona a wave. She waved back, noticing that his son was staring at her.

"You're Rona?" he asked when she approached him.

She nodded. "And you must be Gary."

He gave her a curious look. "You're the house-keeper?"

His question held a note of sarcasm and it took her a moment to sort for an answer. "We'll see."

He shrugged and wrapped his arm around the girl, then steered her toward the boat.

Nick had stepped onto the pier and held the rope, waiting for her to arrive. "Hi," he said, his eyes twinkling in the noonday sun.

"Hi," she said, not knowing how to act being a prospective employee and not his friend. She'd mulled the question and felt at a loss about what he expected. "Thanks for inviting me to look at the apartment."

"It's my pleasure." He clasped her hand and drew her closer. "I hope you don't have other plans. I'd like you to stay for dinner."

Dinner. She looked into his smile and caught her breath. "Do you treat all your employees so well?"

He grinned. "No, but you're different."

Different. The comment puzzled her until she realized not every employee lived at his home. That made her different.

He clasped her arm, then motioned for her to climb into the boat. "Step right there on the footrest and grab that handle."

Rona eyed the spots he'd indicated and slipped her leg over the side of the boat, grasped the handle, then brought her other leg inside while balancing her weight. She relaxed when she had both feet on the floor of the craft.

He hadn't let go of her arm, and before he did, he gave it a squeeze. "Good job." He motioned to the girl. "Amy, it's your turn."

She hopped in as if she'd had lots of practice and sank onto a bench. Amy's long lashes brushed her cheekbone as she gave a lingering look at Gary, who remained on the pier.

"Rona, this is Gary's friend Amy." He turned to the girl. "Amy, Rona."

They nodded to each other as Nick stepped aboard and gestured to Gary to untie the ropes. Nick dropped onto the pilot's seat and beckoned Rona to join him. She slid onto a passenger seat and looked back to see Gary hop on board and settle beside Amy.

The motor revved and Nick guided the boat out into the water. Once they'd traveled a distance, they gained speed and sailed into the lake. The island grew closer and Rona could see more detail. Homes nestled beyond the trees, spacious lawns with large boat-houses, two stories or higher. She could only imagine what living there might be like.

A hand touched her arm and she looked into Nick's shining face. "What do you think?" he said, loud enough for her to hear above the sound of the motor and the waves hitting the hull.

"Wonderful." She couldn't help but smile and enjoy the pressure of his hand against her arm.

His hand dropped as he gestured ahead. "I suppose you know that's Marquette Island. Did you know Les Cheneaux means 'the channels' in French?"

"Bernie told me."

He leaned closer. "Marquette's the biggest. We live on the other side of Cube Point."

She followed his finger along the sweep of land.

"Have you had a chance to tour the lake?"

She shook her head.

"I'll have to take you around. It takes a couple of hours and you'll be amazed."

He turned back to the wheel, occasionally naming some of the small islands as they neared, while she leaned back and enjoyed the breeze whispering through the cabin.

Rona glanced behind her. The wind was stronger there and Gary held Amy in his arms as she leaned against him, his lips nuzzling her hair, his hands running the length of her arm. A smidgeon of envy rolled up her spine and she turned away.

As they rounded the bend, Nick pointed again. "That's Long Island and behind it is Birch Island. My place is in that direction."

Again she strained to see beyond the water to the shore, wondering what his home might look like.

As he cut inward toward the land, the houses became more distinct and finally he slowed. She could see the lovely homes once again—elegant homes, and one of them was Nick's.

He nosed the boat between two lengthy docks and she gazed ahead of her at the sloping lawn that rose to a lovely two-story home built of stone with brown clapboard siding above. The two-story boathouse, built of the same dark siding as the house, butted to the end of a double pier.

Nick helped her from the boat and, though she'd loved the ride over, the wooden planks felt better beneath her feet. He let Gary tie up and grasped Rona's arm as they walked to the end of the dock and finally stepped onto solid ground.

"Let's go up to the house and I'll show you the apartment later."

Nick motioned to an outside staircase that rose to the second story of the boathouse. And though she was eager to look inside, she was nearly as anxious to see inside his house—the place where she would be cleaning and cooking, she guessed.

The hill's incline was steeper than she had imagined and she fell behind Nick, trudging to the top.

"Need a little help?" He turned and offered his hand with a grin. "You'll get used to it."

She grasped his large hand as he drew her to his side. Rona loved the feel of her hand in his, his strong fingers wrapped around hers, the scent of his after-shave permeating the fresh air.

"We're here," he said, releasing her hand when they reached the top of the hill.

She missed the warmth of his touch, yet the sparkle in his eyes remained. "Welcome to Marquette Island." His hand swept a span of property encroached by large evergreens and a few sturdy maples.

"It's beautiful," she said, amazed at the view of the two islands he'd pointed out earlier. "I'll take you up on that ride one day. I'd love to see the islands."

"It's a deal."

He grasped her arm and steered her onto the stone walkway that led to an enclosed porch with rattan furniture. Beside the front door, two side-panel windows gave her a view of a foyer with a broad staircase, an elegant fanlight rose above to the second story. She couldn't imagine even heating the place, let alone paying the mortgage.

Nick pushed open the door and motioned her inside. The first view caused her to gasp. The two-story foyer offered an overlook leading to the second story rooms. She'd never seen anything so lovely.

"Nick, it's lovely." Her voice gushed with awe, and she cringed at the sound.

"Thanks. It's home."

Home. The word settled into her heart. This could be her home, at least for a while. Then she corrected her thought. She would live over the boathouse—an apartment, Nick called it. She knew it could never be this grand.

He moved ahead of her and motioned to a room on his left. "Dining room here. French doors leading to the porch. On a nice day we can open the doors and let the breeze come inside."

French doors. Breeze. She controlled her impulse to gasp aloud.

He cut through the dining room into an open hallway that led in three directions. Ahead of her between three columns, she viewed the family room with a fireplace at the far end, a huge room with sofas and chairs and, near the hearth, a serving counter.

Nick led her to the left where he opened a door to the laundry room, then into the kitchen with its butcher-block island and breakfast-nook alcove surrounded by windows that looked out to the expanse of trees beyond the patio.

"Let's head outside. I want to turn on the barbecue."

Shade sprinkled patterns on the stones. She eyed the umbrella table, log glider and picnic table, stopping at the barbecue pit made from stone.

Nick spilled in the charcoal chips and lit the fire as she stood beside him, feeling the warmth as the heat flared. Yet when Nick faced her, she realized the warmth had permeated her heart as well and had nothing to do with the fire.

"After we eat, I'll show you the rest of the house and the apartment. Gary's anxious to meet his friends in Cedarville, and I promised him he could go."

"Can I help with dinner?"

"I never turn down an offer like that."

A flicker of something deeper flashed in his eyes and Rona wondered if it had to do with her or Gary. She recalled Nick had problems with his son, but today she'd seen no sign, except for the questioning look he'd given her at the marina in Hessel.

When she stepped away from the fire, a chill rippled across her arms.

"Cold?"

"Just a chill. I'll be fine."

"Let me loan you a sweater."

He beckoned her inside where the warmer air ended the chill. "I'm fine. What can I do to help?"

"How about a salad?"

"I can handle that."

He motioned her toward the refrigerator, then pulled a wooden bowl from a cabinet and set it on the counter.

Rona pulled out the salad fixings and went to work, but she couldn't resist watching Nick marinade the thick steaks and butter the baking potatoes before he popped them into the microwave.

When he carried the steaks outside, Rona stopped

a moment to steady herself. This felt too good, too wonderful, to be real. Could she really live here and cook in this great kitchen with everything a chef could want—lots of cabinets, stainless steel appliances, a dishwasher. The mint-green walls with splashes of darker green combined well with the white counters; the natural wood flooring brought the outside in.

Her heart skipped a beat as she heard Nick return followed by the beep of the microwave.

Nick opened the door, slid the potatoes onto a tray and headed outside again. Curious, she peered through the window and saw him slip them onto the grill.

Rona smiled, seeing Nick's comfort in cooking. Maybe she wouldn't be expected to cook their meals. She sliced the last of the tomatoes, then added cucumber and mixed lettuce. She gave the veggies a toss and waited for him to return.

Nick came in and crossed to her, bringing along with him the scent of the charcoal and the fragrance of outdoors. "Croutons in the cabinet over the microwave and cheese in the meat keeper."

"You seem to know your way around the kitchen."

"I have to know that—"

His face darkened and Rona wished she hadn't opened her mouth. "Right. You have a growing teenager to feed."

He nodded but grew silent.

Gary popped his head through the family room doorway. "When are we eating?"

"Soon. Go out and check the steaks."

Gary drew Amy into the kitchen and through the doorway to the patio. She clung to him and Rona wondered what it would feel like to have a man she could lean on. One that she admired and respected; a man she could love.

Love seemed an alien emotion. She'd run away for lack of it and to safeguard herself. She'd had her reasons, but making the move had been harder than she realized. Moving to a town where she knew no one except an elderly woman might have stopped most people, but if they'd been in her shoes, they might have run off, too.

A couple of friends and a father who'd spent most of his lifetime drunk hardly seemed worth sticking around the Detroit area and dealing with her brother again.

Yet she had loved him. They were kin and she knew that should mean something. To him, it meant someone to rip off and manipulate. To Rona, it meant memories of her mother and the familiar, as bad as it had seemed sometimes.

She gave the salad another toss and realized Nick had left the kitchen. She returned the unused cheese to the refrigerator and studied the dressings. Finding two choices, she pulled them out and set them beside the wooden bowl.

Gary darted in and swung open the refrigerator, then stopped. "He has you working already, huh?"

The tone of his comment took her aback. "I volunteered."

"Sucker," he said, pulling out two pops from the shelf. "Grab something to drink for yourself." He slammed the fridge door and vanished outside.

Sucker. Maybe she was, but what she'd seen of Nick she liked, despite her earlier fears. She'd suspected him of being a playboy or thinking she was a loose woman, perhaps, but now she had second thoughts. He'd proven to be kind and she had to go on trust.

Trust. That was a word that had left her vocabulary for so long.

"We're ready."

Nick's voice broke through her unpleasant reverie and she jumped.

"Sorry. I didn't mean to scare you." He gave her a curious look. "Are you ready? We need the drinks and salad."

Rona gathered the salad bowl and dressings.

"Ginger ale or cola?" he asked.

"Ginger ale is fine."

He grasped the drinks, closed the fridge and opened the door. Rona stepped outside, greeted by the scent of grilled steak and the warmth of sunshine. She headed for the picnic table, but when she turned, Nick hadn't followed.

Gary and Amy were at the grill and she watched them until Nick returned and placed a drink in front of her, then wrapped a sweater around her shoulders.

"Just in case," he said. "The sun will be shifting to the front of the house in a while."

The soft knit rubbed against her arms and she fingered the fabric. Cashmere, she guessed, a beige cardigan. She'd never seen him in a sweater, but she knew it was his by the size and the fragrance. She'd already gotten to know his musky scent.

She slipped onto the bench and drew her legs over the seat. Nick settled beside her with Gary and Amy on the other side. As Gary reached toward the steak platter, Nick grasped his hand.

"Let's offer a blessing for the food."

Gary gave him a look between embarrassment and irritation, and Rona had been too surprised to react. Nick was a Christian. She hadn't guessed. He seemed too down to earth and real. Her mind flew back to her church days. She'd been real then, too, but her reality had been difficult and God hadn't offered her any help.

Nick reached for her hand and she placed her palm in his. He closed his fingers over them and gave her hand a squeeze. "Heavenly Father, we thank You for this tremendous day, for sunshine and every blessing. We thank You for food and the company You've brought to this table. Bless this food and us as we enjoy it. In Jesus' name, we pray. Amen."

Rona mumbled an amen, too, surprised it had left her lips, but she was grateful for the company and the food that smelled so appetizing. She hadn't had a home-cooked meal for a week and she knew this would be a treat.

Gary had snagged a steak first, eliciting a glare from Nick, then passed the platter to Amy. Next Nick took the dish and handed it to Rona. She eyed the large steaks looking for one that seemed the smallest. The potatoes, salad and a basket of crusty rolls were next.

They silenced as they delved into the good food. Sunlight beamed against Rona's face and Nick's company warmed her even more. The juicy steak sliced smoothly and melted in her mouth. She enjoyed the buttery potato and the tang of the dressing on the scrumptious salad.

Gary scarfed down the food and as soon as he'd finished, he suggested he and Amy leave. She eyed the rest of her steak but rose with him.

Nick reared upward. "I thought you'd like to visit a while, Gary."

"Why? You told me I didn't have to stick around."

Nick released a sigh. "We have company."

"She's the housekeeper. Since when do I have to be friendly with a housekeeper?"

Rona wanted to stop the fiasco. "It's okay, Nick. I understand. He has plans."

"See your employee is smarter than you are, Dad."

Nick swung his leg over the bench and rose, motioning to Gary to follow him. The boy gave an arched-brow look to Amy, who batted her eyes while Gary followed his dad inside.

Rona eyed the girl, wishing she could break the silence until Amy did.

"Gary's dad doesn't understand what it is to be a teenager."

Rona controlled her frown. "But he was one once, you know."

"That's the olden days. Times are different."

They were, Rona knew, but that didn't make them right. "Love doesn't change."

She screwed up her nose and frowned. "What's that mean?"

"It means Gary's dad loves him and wants the best for him."

"You think so?"

She nodded. "I know so."

Amy gave a shrug. "Gary doesn't think that."

"Maybe you could—"

"Amy, let's go."

Gary's voice surged across them and stopped Rona's comment, probably for the best. "It was nice to meet you."

Amy gave a nod and darted off to Gary.

In a moment, Nick returned and sank onto the bench. "Sorry. It's what I've been dealing with for too long."

She reached out and touched his hand. "It's okay. Kids don't always behave as we'd like. They think they come first and we're just old fuddy-duddies."

He chuckled. "Fuddy-duddies. I haven't heard that expression in years."

"That's because you are—"

"One of them, I suppose."

He laughed and gave her a playful hug.

His touch surprised her. Yet she loved it.

When she looked at his face, she realized he'd surprised himself. "I hope that didn't—"

"You were only teasing."

His eyes brightened. "You're a good sport. And now that you've met Gary, you realize you'll have to be a good sport to work here."

"I'll manage."

His eyes widened. "Then you'll take the job."

She swung her arm toward the front of the house. "I haven't seen the apartment yet."

He grabbed her hand and gave her a playful tug. "Let's get going."

She stepped over the bench and ran along with him, the sun dancing at her feet, the breeze ruffling her hair. She felt free and relieved, the kind of feeling that had long evaded her. They hurried around the corner of the house, Nick still clinging to her hand, and she sprinted beside him down the hill, a much easier journey than going up.

When they reached the steps, he motioned her to go first. She took a drink of air and strode the steps to the landing. At the top she had a bird's-eye view of the house.

Nick pushed the door open, then swooped her into his arms and carried her across the threshold. He lowered her to the ground, his hand sweeping the expanse. "I don't want you to forget your first entry into what I hope will be your home."

He'd startled her with the dramatic entrance, but she agreed with what he'd said. How would she ever forget being in his embrace? She'd felt the ripple of his brawn beneath his knit shirt and the pressure of his broad chest against her arm.

"I won't forget," she said, managing to hide her pleasure. When she had a moment to concentrate, she drew in the scent of lemon instead of dust and felt her mouth drop. Someone must have cleaned and, without a housekeeper, she figured it had to have been Nick. The idea touched her.

Though not as elegant as the house, the apartment was amazing. Terra-cotta-hued walls lent a rich look to the straw-toned trim. The upholstered furniture picked up the earth tones and added splashes of deep gold and rich salmon as did the accessories. The room had a sunny southwest feel that heartened her spirit.

At the far end, she looked out the broad window to the water and the clear view of the two islands and a hook of land off in the distance. The sun lit the lake with golden sparkles dancing on the waves. "It's gorgeous." She turned toward him where he remained at the door.

"A small kitchen is around the corner."

He swung his arm in that direction and stepped forward.

Rona followed Nick past the small round table into the galley kitchen, small but neat and all she needed, with even a microwave and dishwasher.

"You treat your guests well."

"Shouldn't I?"

She shrugged, never having had a special place for guests.

From a door, he beckoned her forward, and that door led to the bedroom and bath. He waited as she stepped inside. Her heart lurched. Sitting on the pillow of the turned-down bed, she saw a chocolate candy wrapped in gold foil.

She eyed Nick and he grinned. "We aim to please."

Rona wanted to hug him. Instead, she scanned the sprawling bedroom with a wonderful walk-in closet—too large for her small amount of clothing—and the bathroom with a shower and tub, everything a woman could want. "Amazing."

"Glad you like it." He stepped closer and rested his hands on her shoulders.

She stood nose to nose with him, wrapped in his scent, and her pulse skipped as she focused on his well-formed lips bracketed by smile creases.

When she raised her eyes to his, she realized he'd been studying her. His probing expression caused heat to creep from below her top to her neck, and though she willed it to stop, the warmth continued to rise. Their eyes locked and it seemed an eternity before she could pull away from his gaze.

"Why do I make you so uneasy?"

His question nailed her. She felt like elastic pulled to its limit and ready to snap. "I'm—" What? What caused her wavering emotion? She liked him. She sensed in the core of her being Nick was a good man, yet she felt as if she were standing on the brink of something. An abyss? Or heaven?

Tears welled in her eyes and Nick's arm wrapped around her and pulled her close. "I didn't mean to make you cry."

She wanted to stay in his arms forever, feeling his chest against hers, his kindness and tender caring. She pulled her head back and looked into his eyes. "It's nothing you said or did. It's me. Things have happened so fast."

She stepped back, reading his expression and fearing he thought she meant he'd come on too fast. "Your job offer. Bernie's offer. I'm not used to so many things working out for the good."

Silence fell over them. The sun drifted through the windows as tiny dust sprinkles danced on the air until they descended to the floor. He'd cleaned the apartment for her and left her the chocolate. She scanned the sunny room, the simple but comfortable furniture, the privacy, the view from the window. Home. These rooms would be her home. "This is almost too good to be true."

"You're happy?"

"Very."

He shifted, leaving more space between them. "Does this mean, yes, you'll take the job?"

"I'd be a fool to say no to a wonderful job and place to call home. Yes. It's perfect."

Chapter Seven

Rona felt uneasy telling Bernie about the new job, but when she did, he only nodded. "I was afraid I'd lose you. You're a good worker, Rona, and if ever you need a job, you're always welcome back here."

"Thanks," she said, raising on her tiptoes to give him a big hug. He smelled of French fries and a hint of his delicious burgers, but she'd learned to love the scent.

"Look, I'll see how fast I can get someone in here. Gerri's been dropping by and apologizing for quitting. I feel sorry for her. She'd had some bad luck lately and I think dropping the tray was the last straw. She's not a bad waitress…if she can keep her moods in control."

Rona touched his arm. "Don't rush finding someone for me."

He tilted his head with a questioning look. "But you want to get out of the motel, I know."

"Nick offered to let me move in as soon as I want. I'll start work for him when I can."

"Really? Or are you just saying that to make me feel better?"

"No, really. I'm going to move over there tonight after work. I need to pick up some groceries and things, but the apartment is furnished with most everything I need."

"Then I'll take the two weeks and see what happens. I might give Gerri a try while you're still here." He chucked her under the chin. "You're a nice woman, Rona. I want the best for you."

She gave him a wink. "You're just trying to charm me."

"Maybe," he said, with a silly grin. "But I think the best man will win."

The best man. She studied his face and caught on. Nick. He thought something was going on. "No way, Bernie. No. It's not like that. Nick's a good man. He's a Christian and not after me. And I'm certainly not looking for a lover or a husband. I had a husband once, and once was enough."

"Not necessarily. You can have a bad steak, but when you get one that melts in your mouth, then you'll love steak again."

"Steak. Somehow it always comes around to food." She gave him a playful poke. "It's time you get some of that food under the warmer."

He chuckled and went back to the grill.

Rona had been astounded that Nick had made her that offer. He said the apartment was empty and rather than her waste money on the motel for two more weeks, she might as well use it. She'd almost said no, but thinking about the lonely nights in the single room, she agreed and hoped she'd made the right decision.

When Bernie called to her, telling her an order was up, Rona loaded the items on her arm and headed for the table. Every time she stepped into the dining room, she scanned the tables, wondering if Nick had come in. Today she had been disappointed.

After refilling coffee, Rona cleaned off a couple of tables and slipped the generous tips in her pocket. The extra money always came as a welcome gift, and when she counted her tips at the end of the night, she'd been amazed to see how quickly her income had grown. Working for Nick would mean no monetary surprises. She'd agreed to her salary and the use of the apartment was appreciated beyond words.

She knew she could eat with the family, too, but it didn't seem appropriate. Gary could come to resent her, and people might talk if they dropped by, so she decided that other than on rare special occasions, she'd cook her own dinners at home.

The clock hands inched as she anticipated the big move at the end of the day. When finally the small hand reached five, there was still no Nick.

When Dolores arrived followed by Mandy, Rona slipped off her apron, ate a bowl of soup and waited at a table out front. The minutes inched by and after waiting so long her neck had begun to ache from craning toward the doorway.

She rose and stepped into the kitchen. "Bernie, I'm going across the street to the market. If Nick comes, tell him I'll talk with him tomorrow."

"But I thought—"

She held up her hand and shrugged. "Plans can change. I'm not going to wait. He said five and it's going on six." Though she sounded noncommittal, she didn't feel that way inside. Her neck ached but not nearly as much as her heart.

When she reached her sedan, Rona tossed her bag onto the passenger seat and slipped inside. After she shut the door, she leaned back and took a deep breath. Life had a way of disappointing her, but she could give him the benefit of the doubt.

She tried to quell her irritation, but couldn't. She started the car and drove toward the piers farther along, angry at herself as she passed the E.S. Mertaugh Boat Works. On the other side of the building, she focused on the boat slips. Nick's boat was there but not Nick. She glanced toward the place he parked his car. His SUV wasn't there. She sped away, turned around when she could and headed to her motel.

Things happen, she kept telling herself. She'd learned that lesson over and over. Her whole life seemed to be filled with things happening, but not the things she wanted.

"I'm so pleased you called," Shirley said, when she opened her front door and pushed aside the screen. "Come in."

Rona stepped inside and gave Shirley a quick hug. The Bailey house smelled, as always, of baked goods and Rona allowed the comfort to wrap around her, controlling her disappointment.

Shirley motioned toward the living room and Rona followed her, settling where she had her last visit.

"Have some tea," Shirley said, pointing to the coffee table where she'd placed a teapot. Her pleasant look took on a concerned edge. "Is something wrong? I heard it in your voice and now I see it on your face."

So much for hiding her emotions. Rona tried to shake her head, but knew the older woman would pry it out of her, probably because she wanted her to. "It's silly."

"Apparently, it's not. And if it's important to you, then it's important to me."

Rona's gaze shifted to the floor, trying to put her thoughts in order. Finally she lifted her gaze. "First, I accepted the job at Nick's."

"Nick's?" Shirley's questioning gaze changed to understanding. "Nick Thornton. The housekeeping job."

"Yes."

"I'm so pleased, Rona. I told you God had a way of working things out."

Not wanting to go there, Rona let her own comment about God stay put in her thoughts. "It includes a lovely apartment."

"So you have a job and a home. That's wonderful." She lifted a teacup from the table beside her. "I will admit I'm disappointed. I would have loved you here, but this is better. God shows us the way."

Rona pursed her lips, then gave up. "Why do you say this is God's doing. It could be just a plain old answer to circumstance. He needed a housekeeper. I needed a job."

Shirley drew back and studied her. "For some reason, I thought you were a believer."

Feeling chastised, Rona struggled for a response.

Tell her the truth or just ignore what she said? Her shoulders lifted as she drew in a deep breath. "I probably was when I was a child."

"But now you're an adult and you know better?"

If she kept talking, Rona knew she would dig herself into a pit. "I don't know anything. I just—"

"I didn't mean to sound harsh." Shirley leaned closer, her face softening to match the gentle look in her eyes. "We all have times when we question God. That's part of being a Christian."

She leaned back against the cushion. "When Sam died, I lived through shock, confusion and anger. I saw people who weren't believers living the high life and my Sam, who was faithful to the Lord, had been taken from me. It didn't make sense."

"That's what I mean. God doesn't make sense."

"God makes sense. He knows His reasons, and what He does has logic, but we just don't understand it because we're not Him."

"We're like puppets, then."

"Puppets have no choices. They make no decisions. People pull a puppet's strings. God gave us choices. He allows us to make mistakes so we draw closer to Him. If everything was perfect, we wouldn't need the Lord. When times are tough, then we come to Him and He hears us."

"So He sets us up for failure so we can come to Him with our faces spattered with filth. That's a loving God?"

"We set ourselves up for failure. He gave you free will. You make choices. If we would only learn to listen to Him, to His Word and to the small whisper in our heart, we wouldn't make bad choices."

"So it's all my fault."

Shirley sent her a gentle look. "It's *our* fault. We don't trust God enough to give Him our whole hearts."

What she said butted against Rona's preconceived notions, each thought banging into the next. "How do you know this?"

Shirley pressed her hand against her chest. "It's in here. When you were a little girl or even now, do you wake up running to the window to see if the sun is still in the sky?"

"No."

"Do you know that spring follows winter, then summer changes to autumn, then winter returns?"

"Yes."

"That's how I believe in God. Because He created the world, and He has kept His promises. He waters the earth. He allows seeds to grow and He guides our steps."

Rona wasn't ready to take the blame for all the horrors that happened in her life. "You're telling me God guides my steps?" She felt her back stiffen.

"The Bible says that a person can plan his course, he can choose what he'll do next. God guides us, but we must listen. The Lord wants us to love Him by choice, not because He makes us love Him. Do you see the difference?"

Nick flew back into her mind. She wanted Nick to care about her because he wanted to, not because she made him. That she understood. So was that the same with God?

Rona nodded her head, her throat tangled in emotion. She wanted to ask Shirley to change the subject, to let her think, but she feared the woman wouldn't stop.

"That's enough," Shirley said. "You have something to think about. Let's enjoy the tea while you tell me what's wrong."

It was as if Shirley had read her mind, and Rona's pulse heightened.

"Are you living on the island now?"

Rona swallowed her emotion. "Not yet. I gave Bernie a two-week notice, but he's already looking, so—"

"Why waste money on a motel, then? Would you like to stay with me for the next two weeks?"

"I was supposed to move to the island today." The words slipped out before she could think to rephrase them.

Shirley's expression changed to understanding. "Supposed to? So that's your problem."

"Something came up."

"You were disappointed. I'm sure you looked forward to getting into your new home today."

Rona felt her head nodding in agreement. "He didn't call, but I'm sure he has a reason."

"I know he does."

How did she know? Her comment grated on Rona's nerves.

"It's trust, Rona. Somewhere along the way you lost trust in people. Now you don't trust Nick or the Lord. Just work on trust. It'll all come back. I promise."

Rona set down her cup and fell back against the cushion. Trust. Nick. The Lord. How did Shirley work her way through a conversation and end up where she started? Rona had no idea what to say. Instead, she glanced at her watch.

"I'd better be on my way. I have a few things to

do yet." Getting away was the main thing. Rona lifted her shoulder bag from the floor and stood, seeing the disappointment on Shirley's face. "Thanks so much for the tea."

"I hope you won't be a stranger."

"No." She embraced the woman. "I'll have time off."

"I'm afraid I scared you away."

"You didn't. I really need to get home."

She rested her hand on Rona's arm. "Then let me leave you with one thought. 'Trust in the Lord and lean not on your own understanding.'"

The words smacked Rona. Shirley had finagled trust and the Lord back into the conversation. She meant well, Rona reminded herself. She turned the doorknob and stepped outside, giving Shirley a wave, then headed for her car hounded by a question.

If she believed she was right, why did Shirley's talk about God and trust bother her so much?

Nick checked the time and leaned against his SUV headrest. He looked at the dark motel room and struggled with the situation. Why had this happened?

Rona seemed sensitive. He knew he'd upset her by not showing up earlier, but it had been out of his hands. He hoped she would understand.

Sometimes Rona grew so serious without any explanation. Yesterday in the apartment, he'd noticed her expression shift from a pleasant expression to a dark scowl. She did that on occasion and he was curious about what triggered the more serious look. He couldn't deny that his own lighthearted feelings sometimes snagged on old memories and unexpectedly changed his mood.

Grateful Rona had accepted the job offer, Nick could only imagine how wonderful it would be to come home to living sounds in the house instead of the creak of a rafter or the skitter of a squirrel on the rooftop. They were lonely sounds and he longed for the day when laughter and happiness filled the house again.

He'd thought about dating. He'd even thought about marriage again one day. Gary needed a mother, but a big question held him back. He'd made mistakes in his marriage to Jill, but he didn't know what they were. He saw her discontent and he had been at a loss to know what to do. Before he could figure it out, he'd seen his wife die with the turn of his head. The memory knifed through his gut.

Another car headed along the highway, but he'd given up hope. Though he knew Rona would have to arrive home soon, he'd waited over an hour and a half and it seemed senseless.

His pulse kicked as the car slowed and pulled into the motel parking lot. Rona. He recognized her sedan. Nick waited until she opened her door before he slid out and headed toward her. She turned to face him, concern on her face, but when she saw it was him, Nick saw her relief.

"I'm so sorry. I know I let you down."

She brushed his words away. "No problem. You don't owe me anything."

"Yes, I do. I owe you my word. I said I'd be there at five."

She slipped the motel key into the lock and opened the door a few inches before she faced him. "I hope you haven't waited long. There was no need."

He rested his hand on her shoulder and searched her eyes. He'd hurt her. She couldn't cover that. "I said it already. I keep my promises, but I had a problem. Can we talk?"

She stood a moment without moving. "Really, Nick. I'm hungry, and I need to—"

"I haven't eaten, either."

She stood with her shoulder facing the door and motioned toward the street. "Then go ahead and have dinner. I'm fine. Shirley Bailey offered me a place for the next two weeks. I can stay there."

Nick grasped both her shoulders and turned her to face him. "Can I come in for a moment? I'd like to explain." He read her expression and decided to get hard-nosed. "I'm not leaving until I talk with you." He released his grip and waited.

Finally she stepped inside and left the door open for him.

Nick followed, scanning the typical motel room, clean but small. One chair and the bed. He motioned to the chair. "Can I sit?"

She gave him a one shoulder shrug. "If you'd like."

He didn't respond but settled into the seat. It seemed obvious to him that someone had hurt Rona so badly that it continued to affect her relationships. The awareness saddened him.

Rona moved away from the chair and stood near the foot of the bed in front of the television set.

"I know you're upset with me."

"I'm fine. I told you."

"I feel bad enough. Could you sit a minute and give me a chance to explain?"

She finally conceded and sank to the edge of the mattress and faced him.

"I had another to-do with Gary, but this time it was serious. He'd skipped school and the police picked him up with some boy I don't know. I had to drive to St. Ignace to the sheriff's department."

"The police?"

"The boys had been drinking and driving, and the other boy ran off the road into a tree."

For the first time, her expression changed. Her eyes darkened with his explanation and he witnessed real concern on her face. "Was Gary hurt?"

"I'm praising God he only had a few bumps and scrapes. I should have called you, but I left so fast I forgot my cell phone."

She moved beside him and rested her hand on his arm. "Nick, don't worry about it. I'm so sorry. And drinking. That's so sad." She leaned closer and shifted her hand to his arm. "So where's Gary now?"

"The officer suggested holding the boys tonight. Gary got a little mouthy and they want to give him a scare. He was so drunk he didn't know what he was doing. They put him in juvenile detention for tonight."

"Is this the first time?"

"The first." Nick's chest ached from holding back his anguish. "But I don't know where Gary's life is going. He's so angry. I'll have to go back tomorrow and pay the bond to bring him home."

Rona looked at him, her eyes rimmed with tears. "You don't deserve this. I'm sure Gary will be sorry tomorrow and I know a night in jail will make the lesson real. It's not a fun place."

She spoke with such conviction it surprised him. "You know about jail?"

A startled expression flashed across her face. "My brother."

Though he wanted to probe, he controlled the urge. "Then you understand."

Rona nodded and a sigh rattled from her. "I hope he learned his lesson."

"Your brother?"

"No. Gary. I hope he realizes what he's done."

"That's my prayer. I'm trying to give it to God."

She looked downward and didn't respond, and it was the first time Nick questioned whether or not Rona was a Christian, but he didn't want to pursue it tonight. He needed to get out from under the pressure he felt in his chest.

Rona's gaze captured his. "I'm sorry I acted rude. I've been disappointed so many times and I guess I fell back into the rut that I've come this far to avoid. Isn't it sad how our troubles follow us?"

Nick understood. He'd let his own worst fears hammer him into the ground too many times. "I want to turn them over to the Lord. I know that's what I'm supposed to do, but I hang on to them anyway. Until we can really let go and give problems to God, they're like anchors around our necks."

"I can relate to anchors." She sent him the first grin he'd seen.

"Are you going to stay with Shirley Bailey or take me up on my offer? It's easier moving only once."

"I didn't commit to Shirley. I—"

"Good. Then hopefully we can make the move tomorrow if all goes well with Gary."

Her look softened and her eyes grew tender. "If not, we can take care of it after you get things settled with Gary. I can stay here another week if necessary."

Nick knew then that she really did understand. "Thanks. They said he'd have a hearing sometime next week." She sat close beside him and he felt almost as if he'd known her forever, though he didn't really know her at all. "Tell me about yourself, Rona."

A painful expression appeared. He didn't want to force her to open up, but he felt impelled to know her better.

She released a sigh. "My mother's dead. My father isn't well. He's been an alcoholic most of his life, as has my brother, who's the one person I want to avoid. I married an alcoholic, unknowingly, and he died in a barroom fight."

Nick hoped he'd managed to keep the shock from his face. She'd spit out her family history in one stream of dialogue without a breath almost, no emotion except bitterness, but could he blame her? "It sounds tough, Rona. I shouldn't have asked."

"I'm working for you. I suppose you have a right to know."

But he saw a difference in her attitude. She appeared to feel stripped of dignity and horribly vulnerable. He longed to embrace her just as he'd done yesterday when she'd gotten teary-eyed. He wanted to let her know that she hadn't been at fault, but she'd clearly considered him only an employer. His probing had put a barrier between them, he feared, and he had no idea how long it would take to open the door again.

"My mom died in a car accident, but my dad, heartbroken, struggled for many years, trying to raise me and a brother who ended up dying in the Middle East. My dad did the best he could. He raised us as Christians and gave us a good work ethic. Yours must have, too."

"My mother did her best. She took me to Sunday school and church, but dad wanted no part of it. Lately, I don't, either."

Her comment threw him. He would never have guessed her attitude toward faith and as his question rose, he felt as insecure as stepping onto a log in a fast-running river. "Can I ask why?"

She didn't respond.

Why had he pushed? "I don't know when to stop, Rona. I'm sorry."

"I don't have an answer, Nick. It's—"

Her voice faded away and whatever she'd started to say she stopped. He'd learned his lesson.

Rona gave him a direct look. "Can we talk about something else?"

Nick agreed, hoping they could recapture their earlier banter, but that wasn't to happen. Not today. Sometimes his foot seemed to head for his mouth without being told to do so. He needed to spend a little knee-time learning how to regain Rona's trust.

Chapter Eight

Rona had been careful not to say anything to anyone about Nick's problem with Gary. If he wanted Bernie and the others to know, it was up to Nick to tell them. He'd called her cell in the afternoon to let her know that Gary was out on bond. He didn't have all the details yet and she could hear the worry in his voice.

Mandy had plied her with questions all day about why she hadn't moved to the island yesterday. She didn't want to lie to her. Even though she'd given up on the Lord, she continued to cling to her Christian upbringing. Paradoxical, she knew, but Christian values were so ingrained in her that she couldn't behave any other way.

Shirley's words about trust and faith kept edging into her mind, with Nick's strong faith adding to the pile of God-stuff she'd pushed aside. She didn't like all the talk about the Lord because it reminded her she'd turned her back on Him and it caused her to think and ask questions. At times, she couldn't even remember why she'd been so determined to pretend God wasn't real.

In her heart, she knew He was, but He'd let her down so badly. Awareness knotted her senses. God had let down Nick, but his faith was as strong as ever. She didn't understand that.

Rona grabbed her tip from the empty table and greeted two new customers who'd come in midday for coffee and Bernie's great pies.

She'd felt antsy since Gary's mess up. Now that she'd accepted the housekeeper job and had seen the apartment, she couldn't wait to get into her own place and enjoy the sense of home she missed so much.

The other thing she missed was Nick.

Since the fiasco with Gary he'd been preoccupied. Though he'd dropped in most days, even if only for a few minutes, she could see his mind was filled with what ifs and worries about Gary. She'd asked how things were going, but he seemed reticent to talk about it and she knew he wanted to keep things as quiet as possible. In a small town that was a mean task.

Mandy skirted past her to clear a table—the busboy had missed work again—but when she came back, she caught Rona's arm.

"You've been quiet. I thought you'd be thrilled leaving this place."

Rona shook her head, surprised that she was a little nostalgic about leaving Bernie even if she'd worked there only a week. "I like it here, believe it or not."

Mandy grinned. "So do I. So what's up?"

"Anxious to move. I feel like I'm biding my time. I'm trying to find things to do. Last night I visited Shirley Bailey and took her a bouquet of flowers."

Mandy gave her a poke. "Salving your guilt?"

"I suppose. She really wanted me to stay with her, but—"

"You don't have to explain. I could live with my folks, too, but I like having a little place of my own. And I mean little. I would have invited you to stay with me, but I didn't think you'd want to share a twin bed."

Rona laughed. "Thanks for not asking."

Mandy's expression changed and Rona turned to see what had caused it. Nick. He looked so drawn and worried.

"I'll let you talk with your boss," Mandy said, sending her a wink that made Rona feel uneasy.

"Just teasing," Mandy said as she scurried away.

Nick headed to a window seat and Rona followed. "You don't need a menu, do you?"

"I have it memorized." He gave her a silly look. "But I hope that'll change very soon."

Rona caught on and tried to put a smile on his serious face. "Did you hire a cook?"

His expression flickered with a faint grin, but it didn't last. He patted the chair beside him. "Have a minute?"

She looked behind her, checking to make sure everyone had been taken care of, then settled onto the chair. "Problems?"

"No. It's too quiet since the fiasco. Last night, I would have been willing to hear the infernal rock-and-roll noise that Gary calls music."

"You need to talk with him even if he doesn't want to."

"But how?"

She shrugged, having no idea, but she knew it had to happen.

"The hearing's next Tuesday."

She leaned closer, noticing the dark circles beneath his eyes. "Tuesday." She slipped her hand along the table and brushed his fingers. "You're worried what will happen."

"I'm trying to stay confident. First offense. I hate to think of him with a record. If only he hadn't mouthed off—"

"Nick, they'll be fair and whatever happens, maybe Gary will benefit. Things happen for a purpose."

He gave her a questioning look and she realized that her faith had put that thought in her head again. What about bad luck? Coincidence?

"You're right." He slipped his other hand over hers and gave it a tender pat, then turned his eyes toward the window as if searching for an answer.

Rona didn't interrupt him. He needed to think and she respected that.

Finally he gave his head a shake as if trying to loosen his thoughts. "I know you've had family problems. What made you leave home?"

"Are you afraid Gary's going to run away?" Or did Nick feel like running away? The question set her on edge.

"No, although I wouldn't put it past him. No, I just wondered, what was the last straw for you?"

The last straw. She wasn't ready to talk about that, but maybe one day. She'd often wondered if she said all those things out loud if it would ease the pain. "I came here on a whim."

"A whim? Without plans?"

"Exactly."

His forehead wrinkled. "That doesn't seem like you."

"It hadn't been, but I…was looking for change. Wanting to find myself. I know that sounds—" she struggled to find a word to describe it "—existential. Weird."

"Existential? That's a hundred-dollar word." His look probed hers.

"I read a lot."

"So do I." He touched her arm. "And what you said doesn't sound off-the-wall or existential to me. I've been trying to find myself for a long time. We have something in common."

Something in common. They had so little in common and she wanted to tell him so, but why? He'd learn soon enough.

Hearing voices behind her, Rona glanced toward the doorway and saw customers heading for a table. "I'd better get to work." She stood and slipped her chair seat under the table.

"Would you like to get moved in on Monday?"

Her heart skipped, and she turned toward Nick's voice. "Monday? Are you sure?"

"Positive. It'll give us time to settle you in before I'm faced with Gary's outcome."

"I know you're worried."

"I am, but I'll feel better knowing you're settled in. Is Monday good?"

"It's perfect."

"Great, and I'll take a cup of that coffee now."

He sent her a full smile that made her day.

The weekend had dragged, and though Nick had dropped in, he'd been tied up with keeping an eye on

Gary. Rona spent the weekend repacking the boxes she'd emptied after the last moving plan had failed. Today she prayed everything would go as planned.

The clock seemed to inch its way toward quitting time. Her car had been packed with her few belongings since yesterday, except for minimal things she needed at the motel for her final night. Today she believed she would really move into her new apartment on the island; and though she had an occasional concern, for the most part the idea lifted her spirit.

When Nick finally came through the door, her pulse galloped. She'd never been so ready for life to begin.

Nick waved and headed toward her. "I know I'm early, but I finished the business I had in town. Should I pack things on the boat?"

She glanced at the clock, noting she had another half hour to work. Rona wanted to leave now, but Bernie had been so good and had already listed the job in the local paper. He told her he had one good possibility and all he needed after that was a new busboy for the dinner hour. If the woman took the job, she'd be free to start working for Nick. She lifted her gaze to Nick's. "I'll get my car keys and you can drive it to the boat. I'll meet you there." She darted to the back for her keys and returned in a moment, handing them to Nick.

He slipped the keys into his pocket. "See you out on the pier." He turned and headed out the door. A few eyes followed his departure, then focused on Rona.

She tried to disguise her smile, but they all knew the story anyway. Everyone who ate at the inn seemed to know everything about everyone. That was the bad part of a small town. She wondered how soon before they all knew about Gary's trouble.

The dinner crowd began to fill the tables and Rona handed out menus and served some guests, then pulled her tips from one of her tables before she slipped into the kitchen and pulled off her apron. She hung it in the storage area and grasped her shoulder bag. "I'm on my way, Bernie."

"Moving to the island tonight?"

She nodded. "Nick's loading the boat now. I'll see you tomorrow."

He slipped a plate under the warmer, then turned to face her. "I'll talk to the woman who filled out an application tonight, and I'll let you know. If she's willing to start work soon, then we won't be bound to the notice."

She crossed the floor and gave him a quick hug. "Thanks, Bernie. You're a good man."

"And you're a good waitress. Remember if this job doesn't work out, you're welcome back." He gave her a wink and she sent him a thumbs-up.

As she walked through the exit, she hoped she'd never have to collect on Bernie's offer. The thought of living on the island in that lovely apartment meant feeling stable and having a real place to call home.

She hurried toward the marina. Noticing her car was gone, she guessed that Nick had moved it to the space near the Linberg cottages across from the water.

Nick saw her when her feet hit the plank walkway to his boat slip. He waved, his ruddy tan heightened in the spring sun and adding to his already good looks. She loved his hair, never slicked back like so many

typical business men. Nick seemed so different—
grounded and real.

She waved back, feeling lighthearted and ready for
a new adventure. Her boxes and luggage were piled
onboard, and Nick was leaning against the hull, looking at some papers. When she drew nearer, he tossed
the clipboard inside and strode toward her.

She waved. "Did I keep you waiting?"

"Only a couple of minutes." He gestured toward the
boxes. "Is this all of it?" His forehead wrinkled with
the question.

"Not much of one's life, is it?"

"We all carry too much baggage. I mentioned a
while ago how we cling to every mess we make. We
need to shed material things and problems." He held
out his hand and helped her step into the craft.

The boat rocked beneath her feet and she balanced
herself, knowing she needed to get sea legs. She'd be
in boats from now on when it was time to come to
town for groceries and— "Nick, I forgot. I wanted to
pick up some groceries for the apartment."

"Don't worry about it tonight. We can take care of
that tomorrow. You can eat with us until then."

She wasn't sure she wanted to do that, but she'd
already received so much from him, lugging her belongings onto the boat and giving her the apartment
early. Instead of arguing, Rona nodded and figured she
could finagle out of it once she was on the island.

She sat in the passenger seat in the cockpit and
watched Nick start the motor and move away from
shore. He kept it slow until he moved farther into the
bay and then picked up speed. This time she knew

where they were going and enjoyed watching Hessel become smaller as the island grew nearer.

When they sailed close to Cube Point, she rose from her seat and made her way outside where the wind whipped through her hair and the sun spread across her arms. When she looked at Nick, he was focused on the point, but he may have sensed she was watching him, because he turned toward her and grinned.

Life hadn't felt so complete in many years. She felt like a child playing house and wondered what it might be like to have Nick as a husband and to be part owner of this boat and the lovely home she'd seen when she'd visited two days earlier.

A week and a day had passed since she met Nick and it felt like she'd known him a lifetime. Was this what it meant to be a soul mate? The idea screeched to a halt in her chest.

Housekeeper. She needed to remind herself. Nick had always been a kind man to everyone. She recalled the day he jumped up to help Gerri when she'd slipped and dropped the food. That's all he was doing for her and she needed to remember that.

They'd swung around the end of Cube Point and Rona tried to envision where the house was in relationship to the vast shoreline. She squinted ahead and finally saw the shape of the boathouse—her home.

With good thoughts in her mind, she moved back to the shelter of the cabin and to Nick. "I hate to admit this, but I'm excited."

"Why hate to admit it? But I want to warn you, with these new problems with Gary, you may want to skedaddle back to Bernie's. I have no idea what's in store."

She didn't like the sound of his comment. "Are you afraid I can't handle it?"

"No. Not at all. I'm thinking you won't want to. Sometimes I wish I didn't have to, but then I feel guilty. I'm his father and I know there's a solution somewhere. I just haven't found it."

Rona understood the feeling. She'd spent the past few years looking for a solution to her troubles, and she could only hope this was the right answer.

They quieted. The sound of the motor and lapping waves infringed on the quiet, but not as much as the worries they both had. She'd sounded confident with Nick just now, but could she handle a teenage boy? She hadn't been able to cope with a brother only a couple years younger than she was. What did she know about teenagers?

The boat slowed as they neared the shore and Nick called her to his side. "Want to learn how to pilot this thing?"

"The speedboat?" She felt panicky. "I thought I'd have a smaller boat."

"You will, but you never know if an emergency arises. Come here." He beckoned her to his side and she went, but not without trepidation.

He slid from the seat and motioned for her to sit, then he stood behind her and wrapped his arms around her from behind. "Grip the wheel."

The heat of his body and the scent of his fragrance heightened her crazy thoughts. "It's like driving a car, just head the prow toward the house."

She clinched the wheel as if her life depended on it, and, to her, it did.

"Ease up," Nick said, lifting one hand and then the other to loosen her fingers. "You don't grip your car's steering wheel like that, do you?"

"No, but—"

"I'll take over when we get close. I won't let you down." He rested his hand on her shoulder and gave it a squeeze.

His fingers felt warm through her cotton top and it gave her a feeling of companionship. She sensed her body relaxing and enjoyed the feel of being in control. It was a feeling she'd lost until recently.

"That's it," he said close to her ear. "Enjoy yourself."

She chuckled at his comment and his voice whispering against her ear. She scrunched her cheek to her shoulder and Nick drew back.

"Sorry. I hadn't meant to tickle you."

Rona turned her face toward his and saw a glint in his eye. Their noses nearly touched and once again her heart raced to her throat with a deep longing to kiss his welcoming lips. She managed a smile to let him know she didn't believe a word of it.

"My turn," Nick said, as they drew closer.

He took the wheel while she slid out from beneath his arms. The warmth vanished from her body but not from inside. Rona hadn't felt this much happiness in a long, long time.

Nick pulled to the dock and tied the lines while she waited, eager to get into her apartment and to begin making it her own.

"I'll teach you how to tie up another day," he said. "I don't want to overwhelm you with my brilliance all in one day."

His silly expression made her laugh.

Nick held out his hand to help her from the boat. She'd begun to get the knack of it and felt more secure. He went on board and stacked the boxes and luggage onto the wooden planks, and Rona grasped a box and headed toward the apartment.

"I'll get those," Nick said as he stepped from the craft with more boxes. He motioned toward the guest-house. "Go ahead and I'll bring these up."

She didn't listen. Instead Rona grabbed one of the smaller bags and headed to shore. She turned to the flagstone walk and climbed the stairs, aware that this was home. She would walk these steps many times before she had to leave.

Before she had to leave. The words smacked against her heart. At this moment Rona never wanted to leave. The comment sounded ludicrous because she'd known Nick for such a short time, but she had the feeling she'd known him forever. He was that kind of person, so open, so kind and generous, so wonderful.

With the thrill of having her own place again, she turned the knob and shoved open the door. The lemony scent she'd smelled days earlier still lingered on the air. She rolled the luggage into her bedroom and hurried back to the front room window to look down at the speedboat. Nick had vanished, but then she heard him behind her.

"Where do you want these?"

She cast a flailing gesture. "Anywhere. I have to open them to see what's inside."

He set the box beside the lamp table and headed out again. This time she watched him on the dock, setting three boxes into a pile and hoisting them in his arms. Even from the distance, she could see his muscles flex, and it sent a spiraling sensation to her stomach.

Rona faced the truth. She needed to get a grip on her emotions or she would be out of a job sooner than she wanted. Nick was her employer. She had to keep saying it over and over in her mind, because her fantasy led her in directions that could be her downfall.

Not wanting to get caught ogling, Rona headed for the last stack of boxes and opened the top one. Shoes and handbags. She carried them into the bedroom, noticing the chocolate candy, as Nick dropped another three boxes onto the floor. She recognized the sound. Books. She'd brought some of her favorites with her. They'd been her solace and she couldn't stand to leave them all behind.

As she opened more of the boxes, Nick returned with the last carton. She'd found some dishes and kitchen utensils, things she probably wouldn't need in this well-equipped apartment.

Nick collapsed on the sofa and tossed his head against the cushion. He released a sigh, and Rona drew closer. "I'd offer you a pop, but I'm not sure which box I put them in."

He grinned and motioned to the refrigerator. "I'd love one. I stocked a few for you."

Thoughtful. The word billowed in her mind. "Thanks." She saw a mix of cola and ginger ale. He'd remembered. She pulled out a cola for him and carried it to him along with a can of ginger ale for herself.

She handed him the drink, then sat in a nearby chair and opened the can, hearing the snap and fizz. When she took a lengthy drink, she realized she'd look more ladylike with a glass.

Nick rested his elbows on his knees, the can clutched in his hands. "I hate to go home."

"Gary?"

"He's sick today. I hope it teaches him a lesson about alcohol. I should have made him go to school, but I didn't."

"Should haves are a waste of time. Now is important. Think of what you'll do to improve the situation."

"If I only knew. I want to be his friend. I want to—"

"Be his dad, Nick. He already has friends."

Nick lifted his gaze and studied her.

"A woman of wisdom."

She watched his fingers run along the side of the pop can as if weighing her words, and she wasn't sure if his comment was facetious or genuine.

"Thanks," he added, answering her question.

"I'm not trying to meddle."

His head tilted up and her heart melted with his look. "You're not meddling. I hope you realize that you'll be dealing with Gary, too, when I'm not here. He'll be your headache as well, and the more I think of it the more I wonder how wise this was."

"I thought you said you believed I could handle the situation."

He straightened, his gaze anchoring hers. "I do, but I like you too much."

Too much. She tried to grasp his meaning. She knew he liked her, and she loved that, but—

"You don't understand," he said.

"I—"

He rose and moved toward her, drawing her from the chair. He closed his eyes a moment and drew in a lengthy breath. "I don't know how to say this, but I feel as if we've been friends forever. Do you believe in that? Do you think it's possible for two people to be on the same wavelength, the same frequency? Like soul mates?"

She'd felt that way herself and thought she'd gone crazy. "I do understand."

"It's as if we landed on an island. Gilligan's Island maybe, and I don't want to be rescued. I enjoy your company. I really like being with you."

Rona felt she had been rescued…by Nick.

Her voice caught in her throat and she only nodded. "I like you, too, but we barely know each other. Once we face each other's idiosyncrasies, we could feel differently. We'd be disillusioned and I don't want that."

He grasped her shoulders. "I know, but I don't think that will happen. I'm—"

"Shush. Let's just get to know each other. Let me do my job, and we can—"

"Pray about it." He studied her face. "Do you pray, Rona?"

He'd kicked her in the stomach. She bit the inside of her lip, knowing at this moment she would disappoint him again. "You know how I feel. I've prayed a great deal of my life and God doesn't hear my prayers, so what's the point?"

"Persistence. Faith. Trust."

"I had that once."

"Then it's still there, but tangled in your flotsam. Do you know that God doesn't always say yes?"

She knew that, and how she knew that. "But He could."

He shook his head. "No, then we'd be without free will. We couldn't make choices. We'd be His prisoners and not His children."

Rona had heard the same lecture from Shirley. She hadn't wanted to talk about it then and she didn't want it to ruin the happiness she felt now.

Nick didn't wait for a response. "Gary always accuses me of treating him like a prisoner. Maybe that's the problem. I want him to be my son, not a prisoner." He looked deeply into her eyes. "God wants the same for us."

She wanted to respond, but she had nothing to say. He'd thrown her with his feelings and then with his explanation. She looked at him a long time before she spoke. "I'll be happy to cook dinner for you tonight."

Her shift in topic threw him for a minute. She saw it on his face. "That would be nice. Gary's home and I can't go out to eat. I put him on house arrest except for school."

House arrest. Prisoner. The vision pelted Rona's conscience. Gary needed love and punishment. He needed both.

"I suppose I've contradicted myself just now, but he's my prisoner until tomorrow. Then I'll take stock of what happens at the hearing."

She clamped her mouth closed, willing herself not to interfere. Housekeeper. I'm the housekeeper.

Chapter Nine

Nick lay in bed all night asking the Lord what to do about Gary. As he tossed from one side to the other, he recalled the story of the prodigal son and what his father had done. Instead of punishing him, since he'd already punished himself by his behavior, the father had opened his arms and thrown a party.

Although Nick wasn't ready to throw a party, he weighed what he could do that would have a similar affect. He still needed some kind of recompense, but he'd wait and see what happened on Tuesday.

He slipped his legs over the edge of the mattress and sat on the bed, listening. He could hear the shower running down the hall. He'd left his door open just to keep an eye on Gary if he'd awakened in the night. Relieved that his son had gotten out of bed without a hassle, Nick rose with a spring in his step and headed for his own shower.

Letting the water wash over him, he cleansed his heart as well and prayed for a brighter day for all of them. Rona had troubled him, too, with her attitude toward the Lord, but he sensed that somewhere inside her God's light still shined and he'd have to be patient and find the match that could light the flame.

He had strong feelings for Rona, and each time he admitted it to himself he experienced disbelief. What had it been? A week? Two weeks? How could he let his emotions loose in so short a time after having clung to them so tightly since Jill had died?

Nick finished his shower, amazed that he smelled coffee and bacon drifting up from the kitchen. Rona. She'd come over to prepare her breakfast. He'd promised to take her shopping today, but he wished she'd just eat with the family. He'd try to encourage that.

Dressed, Nick headed down the stairs and when he neared the kitchen, he heard voices. "Something smells wonderful," he said, walking through the doorway.

Gary sat at the breakfast table, and Nick strode in that direction without making a fuss over Rona. He didn't want to give his son any fodder for gossip. "Looks good," he said, eyeing Gary's scrambled eggs, bacon and toast along with a glass of milk.

"I poured your coffee," Rona said from behind him.

Nick turned toward her as she approached him with a steaming mug. "Thanks. It's great to wake up to food cooking."

Rona didn't say anything and returned to the counter.

Nick slipped into a chair and sipped his coffee, watching Gary out of the corner of his eye.

When Gary pushed back his plate, Nick spoke. "I'll pick you up. What time are you out today?"

"I have exams all day."

"I know. What time will you be done?"

"Two." He looked away, then looked into Nick's eyes. "Two-thirty. I have to clean out my lockers."

"Okay. I'll be there."

As he finished the sentence, Rona set a breakfast plate in front of him, then returned with toast fresh from the toaster. He looked up at her and smiled, but she only gave a nod and stepped away again. Had she eaten? He wanted to ask, but today wasn't the day to fraternize with the new housekeeper.

"Dad, do you have to treat me like—"

"Apparently I do." He glanced toward Rona, but she'd slipped from the kitchen, giving them time alone. "When trust is broken, it's not easy to repair it. Remember that. Now you have to earn trust."

"You're not perfect, Dad."

"No, I'm far from perfect, but I haven't broken my trust to you." Muscles in his shoulders knotted with Gary's attack. He sensed his son had something on his mind. "Get on with it. What's bothering you?"

Gary looked down at his empty plate and shook his head.

"If you have something to say, then say it. Get it out in the open."

"Mom."

"Mom?" His head reeled with the look on Gary's face.

"Maybe mom didn't trust you or she wouldn't have died. She wasn't happy. She used to cry when you weren't home." His face jaw ticked with tension.

"Gary, I didn't know." Nick's voice caught in his throat. But why hadn't he known that? Why hadn't Jill talked with him? What was she hiding? Had it been something he'd done?

Without commenting, Gary rose and hurried from the room, leaving Nick shocked by the comments. Was this why his son had been acting out? The accident had been three years ago and Gary's attitude had changed the past two years. Or had he missed that, too?

Nick lowered his face in his hands and tried to think back. He remembered Gary had been quiet after his mother's death and he'd thought that had been part of the grieving process. He should have taken Gary to a counselor. He should have— "Should haves" filled his mind. The past was over. He needed to do something now to make a difference.

When he lifted his eyes, Rona leaned against the counter, watching him. "Problems?"

He nodded, not wanting to talk with Gary around. She didn't probe and Nick was grateful. He lifted the mug and sipped the lukewarm coffee. His appetite had slipped away and now he looked at the food with little interest, but Rona had prepared it for him and he wanted to try and eat something.

When her hand reached in front of him, he focused on her. She carried the plate to the microwave and popped it in. "I'll warm it. Maybe you can eat a little," she said. When the beep gave its signal, Rona returned his plate to the table.

She grasped his mug and carried it away while the scent of bacon and eggs livened his appetite enough to take a forkful. "Thanks." Thanks for being here. Thanks for offering wise thoughts. Thanks for everything. The simple words couldn't tell Rona how much she meant to him, especially now when he felt so alone.

The situation had flattened him. He considered himself strong and able to deal with every possible business confrontation, but when it involved his personal life, he'd crumbled and that troubled him.

The fragrance of fresh coffee wafted around him as Rona handed him the cup. "I'll go back to my apartment and come down when you're ready to leave. I think you need private time with Gary."

"Thanks. We'll be gone soon. You won't be late for work. I promise."

Rona always had the best solution to a situation. He needed to pray and to think. Gary's accusations knifed him. What had he missed? Had Jill been so unhappy that she'd taken her own— No. Not Jill. A Christian had places to turn. Jill had— He reeled with his thoughts.

On Tuesday, Bernie told Rona he'd found a waitress. She heard the news with a mixture of relief and sadness, leaving Bernie and her co-workers, but she felt certain she'd remain friends with them and that felt good.

At the end of her shift, she hugged everyone, then walked to the pier ready for her new job. Nick had given her a hug when she told him she was now officially his employee. Though it sounded good, she'd begun to think of herself more as Nick's friend and confidant.

Today, Rona had spent the morning setting up her cleaning schedule. She'd divided cleaning various rooms into days, plus finding time for laundry. She would prepare breakfast and dinner daily when the family was home. Nick worked late some evenings and hopefully he'd let her know when he'd be gone. Nick had been on her mind all morning.

Though Nick had told her to take today off, she'd spent some time in the house, locating the cleaning equipment and preparing for the next day's work. Now she stretched her legs farther on the sofa, sipped her iced tea and stared out the window until her back ached, waiting for Nick to arrive home from Gary's hearing.

She pulled her gaze from the windows and eyed her new home, still seeing the shine on the tables. Nick had done a great job for her. She hoped she could please him—please Nick *and* Gary—as much.

A motor hummed to the dock and she rose to peek out the window. They were back. From above she had a difficult time reading the expressions on their faces. From the distance, Nick appeared unsmiling and Gary walked with his head hanging.

Rona stepped away to avoid being seen. She hoped the hearing worked some kind of a miracle for Gary. Miracle. Since when did she think about miracles? She could have used a few in her life.

Hearing her caustic comment, Rona felt remorse. Nick's confidence in God made her ashamed that she had been so down on her faith. He'd been right yesterday when he told her God didn't always say yes. Good parents had to say no to their children sometimes to help them grow spiritually and sometimes to help them to become more appreciative.

Rona had spent a long time feeling sorry for herself, sorry for her situation, sorry for her family—except for her mother. Her mother had been a blessing. Miracle. Blessing. The words came so naturally to her since she'd come to Hessel. Nick's influence. His faith came so easily to him, it seemed. It affected his actions and how he treated others. She'd seen it the first day she'd met him and many days since.

Listening for sounds on the stairs, Rona crossed the room to the window and saw Nick and Gary heading into the house. Her shoulders slumped when they vanished inside. She'd thought Nick would come up and tell her what happened.

"Get a grip," she told herself. How easy it was to forget she was an employee and not a friend. No one ran to tell their housekeeper the news except on TV sitcoms.

Rona lifted her glass from the table and rinsed it at the kitchen sink. She looked at the wall clock and leaned against the counter to think. She had to begin dinner in an hour, unless Nick had other plans. She could run over and ask or at least call him on the intercom she'd discovered her first day in the apartment.

Using wisdom, she returned to the sofa and picked up a magazine. Though she didn't stop to read the articles, she hoped the activity would keep her from doing something stupid, like infringing on Nick's time with Gary.

When she'd finished the magazine, she stood and searched for the TV remote. As she moved across the room, a tap sounded on the door and her stomach flipped. She spun around and strode to the door, hoping to conceal her emotion.

Nick stood on the landing, a flicker of hello in his eyes.

"How'd it go?" she asked, pushing open the screen door.

"Better than it could have."

She motioned toward the sofa. "I'm relieved."

He stepped inside. "So am I. It won't be easy. Gary's so withdrawn. I think he's ashamed, but he's covering it with quiet belligerence." Nick sank into the sofa cushion and looked at the floor.

"Hopefully, that will pass." She wanted to ask details, but she gave Nick time to calm his spirit.

Finally he lifted his head. "I prayed so hard and this time the Lord said yes."

The Lord said yes. Nick deserved a yes. Rona joined him on the sofa but kept her distance.

"The judge gave him a fine that I paid, but he gave Gary two stipulations. First he has to pay the fine. He's been ordered to get a job for the summer and turn the money over to me until it's paid back. When I hand in his pay stubs and vouch he's paid the fine, then his earnings from then on are his."

"That sounds great. Gary's sixteen. He needs to learn to work."

"I know, and I've never asked him to, but—"

"But he will now," Rona added, giving his arm a squeeze. "You wanted him to enjoy the summer, but he will. He'll still have plenty of time to have fun."

Nick nodded.

Curious, Rona waited for him to continue, but Nick only sat in silence. "And the second stipulation?"

His face brightened. "This one I'm grateful for. Gary has to do twenty hours of community work. Our church has teen service projects where the kids volunteer their time at the church and in the community. It's perfect. We dropped by on the way home and our pastor will work with us on that. Gary wasn't too happy about telling Pastor Al, but he finally agreed, and I'm comfortable with that. At least Gary will be using time helping others and getting together with some of the church teens."

"Both conditions sound like a blessing to me." Blessing. The word popped out again.

Nick looked at her as if he'd noticed. He reached out and rested his hand on hers. "Thanks for listening. I don't want to talk about this with everyone, although I'm sure the whole town will know about it soon enough."

"It's not your sin, Nick. Sins of the fathers. Sins of the son. The Bible teaches that one doesn't condemn the other. Each person is responsible for his own sin."

He straightened as if surprised at the biblical references. She'd startled herself, too. She knew the Holy Spirit had His ways. She'd opened the door a crack and the Spirit had wheedled inside her.

"So what happens now?"

"Tomorrow Gary needs to look for work, and I want to find a way to get closer to him." Nick rose. "I've bored you enough."

She stood, too, as he headed for the door. "You haven't bored me, and I'll be in shortly to get dinner ready."

"You don't need to worry about that tonight. I think we'll go over to Harbor Inn for dinner. I don't want to sit here all night with Gary in silence." He stepped closer to her. "Join us."

"No. You two go alone. I'll fix something here."

He studied her face. "Are you sure?"

"Positive."

Nick took a step forward, then turned and put his

hand on the knob, but before he opened the door, he faced her again. "Would you mind if I hugged you?"

"Hugged me?" Her heart revved into a fast gear.

He nodded. "Do you mind?"

Being held in Nick's arms had been her dream. She shook her head and moved forward. "I don't mind at all."

He opened his arms and she stepped into his embrace. He drew her closer and lowered his face into her hair.

She felt his shoulders relax and his tension subside as they stood together in silence. Rona tightened her arms around him, her mind soaring as warning signals flashed. She closed her mind to the warning, then drew in the scent of wind in his hair and the touch of his hand against her back. Nick needed to be loved by his son.

Everyone needed to be loved.

Chapter Ten

Friday, Rona consulted her schedule and cleaned the upper rooms of the house—Nick's office, a guest bedroom and Gary's room. She'd discovered one large room over the downstairs storage room that would make a perfect game room for Gary. Nick had mentioned wanting to find things to do with his son and buying a foosball table or a pool table might be just the thing.

But her grand thoughts of creating a room for Gary and his friends vanished when she cleaned his room and found a book of matches and some cigarette ashes dropped on the carpet. She didn't remember seeing a friend at the house, so she had to assume the ashes were Gary's. Along with drinking, he'd added smoking to his list of negative behaviors.

Maybe Nick was right. Being the housekeeper put her in a bad position, not only dealing with Gary, but trying to decide what to do about the things she stumbled on that she'd have to tell his father.

Rona set the problem on a shelf. Giving it time might be the best. Now that Gary had gotten into trouble with the law, he might be more thoughtful about his behavior. Rona hoped she'd see a change. If she could talk to the previous housekeeper, she'd be able to ask what she'd run into and what she did about it. Nothing, she guessed, since Nick hadn't mentioned Gary's smoking or drinking until the accident had brought it to his attention.

She stored her cleaning gear and pulled a soft drink from the refrigerator. Tomorrow she'd work in the family room and tackle some laundry. Today her work was done, except for preparing dinner.

After setting her drink on the table. Rona wandered to the family room, standing between the two large columns that served as the room's entrance. The archway was different and appealing. On the first day she'd arrived, Rona had admired this large room. It appeared lived-in and purposeful. She liked the serving bar that connected the room to the kitchen and the fireplace bordered by two windows.

She stepped through the columns and walked around the room, stopping at the fireplace mantel. She noticed the furniture needed dusting and so did the fireplace. Her gaze drifted along the mantel, admiring the candlesticks, then seeing photos of Gary when he was younger and one of Gary and Nick. Her gaze faltered over a spot that was dust free—the size of a picture frame. She speculated, but let it drop.

She moved to the window and looked outside into the spacious backyard surrounded by trees, dark leaves and some flowering branches that gave the landscape an ethereal glow.

For the first time, she spotted a lovely old secretary desk. She lowered the lid and eyed the pigeon holes with flowery note paper and feminine trinkets. Jill's desk. She eyed the envelopes, longing to read the letters, then forced herself to close the lid. Instead, she pulled open the drawer. An address book lay to one side and a photograph turned facedown rested beside it.

Curious, she lifted the frame and her heart plummeted. An attractive woman with a bright smile looked at her. Jill. She could see Gary's face, except for his coloring. Jill had reddish blond hair and Gary's was more a light brown like his dad's.

Feeling uncomfortable looking through Jill's desk, she replaced the photograph and closed the door. Nick must have put it inside, but why? She stood a moment, trying to find reasons, then let it go.

When Nick and Gary arrived home, she'd deal with dinner. Until then, her time was her own. She left the house and hurried back to her apartment.

Nick caught the mooring lines and tied them to the piling, then bounded off the dock and took Rona's stairs two at a time. He rapped on the door and when she didn't answer, he realized she was probably in the house.

He'd nearly reached the bottom step when her door opened.

"Nick?"

He pivoted on one foot and darted back up the stairs, unable to control his smile.

Rona's face was knitted with a question and he didn't wait to be invited in. He grasped the screen door handle and darted inside. "I can't believe how things have gone." He drew her into his arms and spun her around before he could stop himself. She'd felt like a feather in his grasp.

When he lowered her to the ground, Rona gazed at him wide-eyed. "I hope this is good news."

Nick laughed at her playful comment. "It is." He'd been about to apologize for the exuberant spin, but her flushed face and playful comment canceled his need to say anything.

She clasped her hands together. "So tell me."

"Guess where Gary found work."

Her brows bent to a thoughtful frown. "Church?"

"No." He couldn't help but chuckle. "Harbor Inn."

"You're kidding."

"Bernie needed a busboy and part-time dishwasher. He starts tomorrow afternoon. Pastor called my cell and invited Gary to put in some volunteer hours there in the morning."

She grasped his arm. "Work and church all on one day?"

"They have a spring-cleaning project going at the church." He pressed his hand against hers. "You know what? Things couldn't have worked out better."

Rona looked at his hand and eased hers away. "I'm sure you're relieved. That's good news."

As she stepped back, Nick got the message. He'd moved too quickly. Not wanting to scare her away, he had to control himself and slow down. These unexpected sensations had been overwhelming and new to him. He'd tried to decipher what had made a difference since Rona appeared in his life.

Why had he been so drawn to her? She had been friendly, nothing more, but maybe, just maybe— All he could do was hope and pray for God's guidance. If she never had feelings for him— The possibility smacked against his chest. Still, he wasn't ready to give up. All good things took work and patience.

The thought made him think of his son. That was another place he needed to put his effort without being discouraged.

"I'd better go back. I need to spend time with Gary."

"You do," she said, stepping toward the door.

He followed with his mind swaying between the relationship with his son and with Rona. He turned back to her. "But tomorrow Gary's busy all day. What do you say about a boat lesson?"

She backed away, her face draining of color. "I— I'm so nervous." She fiddled with the collar of her flowery blouse.

"You don't want to be stranded here, do you?"

Her eyes dart from side to side before she looked at him. "No, but I keep hoping that—"

"What?" Seeing her expression, he had to comment. "That a boat chauffeur would always show up to take you to town?"

She laughed, too. "Yes, but that would be you, I guess, or Gary, and I know that's not always possible." She lifted her shoulders and let them plop. "Okay. Since I must, tomorrow's as good a time as any."

He gave her arm a squeeze, recalling how he'd just held her so close in the giddy unexpected spin. "We'll make a day of it."

"But what about the house?"

He chucked her under the chin. "Everyone needs a day off. It'll be fun." He opened the door and bounded down the steps, his heart surging with adventure and hope.

Saturday morning, Rona changed clothes three times before she found something to wear. She'd dressed in shorts, then felt too exposed. Her boss was showing her how to maneuver the boat, not sun on the beach. Her jeans seemed too casual. She cleaned house in those. Finally she settled on royal-blue Capri pants and a blue-and-red striped top—not nautical exactly, but as close as she could get.

Nick had taken Gary to town for the day and she expected him back soon. Her breakfast had been cereal she'd had to force down and Rona couldn't tell if it was excitement or fear of running the boat that motivated her edginess.

She leaned against the window, looking out at the lake and eyed the distance. No boat heading this way. She sank into the edge of a chair, listening for the sound of the motor and chastising herself for being so ridiculous.

Rona was confident Nick liked her, she had no question about that. He seemed comfortable talking with her and even getting playful. Yesterday, when he'd grasped her and spun her around, her feet had lifted from the floor and he'd set her down before she knew what had happened. Though he'd startled her, she guessed he'd startled himself. Still, she'd enjoyed the strength of his arms around her and seeing him really happy for once.

Rona pictured his exuberance, remembering that her longing to find someone like Nick had grown. No, it had nothing to do with finding someone like Nick. She longed to have Nick fall in love with her. The whole idea was preposterous and impossible. She'd never fit into his world, and he'd never respect her once he'd learned about her problems back home.

So often she relived the scene. Don's request had seemed so simple. "Hey, sis," he said, in his manipulative way, "if you give me a ride to Eastpointe, I can give you back the money I borrowed." Her brother had borrowed so much money from her and the ride had seemed simple enough.

The big question popped from her mouth. "Where are you getting that kind of money?"

He'd given her one of those "don't ask" looks and finally tossed his hands in the air. "I bet on the numbers. It paid out big."

She shook her head. "The numbers, Don. Is that where all the money I've loaned you has gone?"

He waved her question away. "One ride and I'll pay you back."

She'd given in, and her life fell apart from there. She'd been conned by the best con man she knew. Don.

A motor hummed below her and Rona twisted on the seat and looked down toward the water. Nick tied up the boat and before she could find her shoulder bag, he'd reached her door.

"Ready?" he asked through the screen.

Seeing his good looks, her voice caught in her throat. She nodded, then stepped onto the landing beside him and pulled the door closed.

Each day his tan deepened and today his honey-bronze skin glowed a little more. His brown hair had taken on sunny highlights, but the same twinkle brightened his eyes. She'd loved that twinkle from the first day they'd met.

She reached for the door key and Nick covered her hand.

"Who's going to break in on an island? It makes people feel safer maybe, but I just don't bother. It's wasted effort."

She eyed the key, then slipped it back into her purse. He was right, but she wondered if she'd ever feel totally safe.

Nick motioned her down the steps, but when they reached the ground, instead of stepping onto the planks, Nick opened the side door into the boathouse. The shadow inside sent a damp chill across her arms.

"We're taking the runabout," Nick said stepping inside.

Runabout. Not the big speedboat. A whisper of relief whooshed past her. When she stepped into the gloom, blue water twinkled at her from the open end of the covering. She thought about her cozy apartment above this dank space, but it didn't dim her appreciation. No matter what was below her, the sun shone above.

The idea spread over her and prodded her optimism. No matter how gloomy her life had seemed, sunny days waited around the corner. She thought of the Lord in heaven looking down on her and shaking His head while asking how long, my child, did it take you to realize that I am here?

"Rona?"

His voice jerked her attention to the boat.

"Step in." He gave her a look as if asking where she'd been.

For that fleeting moment, she didn't know. She felt as if a voice had spoken to her and the whole idea muddled her. Nick offered her his hand and she clasped it as she stepped into the smaller boat. His hand gave her confidence, but he let go and flagged her forward.

"Sit at the wheel."

She looked ahead to the opening into the lake. He wanted her to steer the boat out of the boathouse. She'd knock down the walls.

Rona gave him a questioning look, a helpless look, she was sure. He only grinned and nodded. She inched her way to the steering wheel, realizing for the first time the wheel was opposite from a car. The boat rocked beneath her feet and she plonked into the seat.

"Good," he said, untying the final rope and stepping inside. He settled beside her and leaned closer, pointing to the shift control. "It's in Neutral, so push the starter."

Rona followed the direction of his finger to the button and pressed it. The motor kicked over and made a soft putt-putt noise. She looked at Nick for direction and he leaned across her and explained how the throttle and choke worked. From the passenger seat, he demonstrated how to shift forward.

When they began to move, to her relief, Nick turned the steering wheel away from the pier, then through the opening into the water.

"Now adjust the throttle," he said.

Rona edged it upward.

He leaned back. "It's time you take the wheel," he said, motioning her to take over.

She did as he asked, and he rested his hand on hers, guiding the wheel in one direction and then another. "See what happens? It's like the speedboat, but easier because it's smaller."

"It is," she said, distracted by the feel of his hand against hers. The sun beat on her skin and the scent of water and sun mixed with Nick's musky aftershave. Her stomach tightened with the sensation.

"Now you take it alone." Nick lowered his hand but remained so close her arm swept against his when she moved the wheel.

She could see the bend of the island and recognized Cube Point. "Am I heading toward Hessel?"

"As good a place as any." He brushed her arm with his fingertips and a shiver coursed through her.

Stop it, she said in her head. She felt mushy inside and the feeling had to stop. Maybe she should call him Mr. Thornton. The formal name might keep her jangled nerves from tempting her imagination.

"You're doing great," he said, slipping deeper into his own seat.

They both settled into silence covered by the sound of the motor's roar and the wind whipping past their ears. Rona's confidence grew. As long as they were alone on the lake, she realized nothing could happen, but as she guided the boat around Cube's Point and saw Hessel in the distance, her assurance waned.

She gave a frantic look toward Nick, but he didn't

come to her rescue. "Just slow up when you get closer to shore. That's regulations anyway."

"Regulations?"

"Good boating. Be kind to your neighbor and avoid a large wake."

She understood and slowed, then headed the prow toward the Hessel marina, frightened but amazed at her sense of freedom.

"After we dock, I want to take a ride to the church."

"The church?"

"Gary'll need a ride to his new job. If he's ready, we can drop him off. Maybe have lunch."

Church? She felt her pulse kick in. *Lord, You are so determined.* It's just like Shirley said. Jesus searched for even the dumbest lambs and brought them back to the fold.

Chapter Eleven

Nick feared he'd pushed too hard on the spiritual issue. He knew where his heart was headed, but he needed to make sure he and Rona were on the same spiritual track and, right now, he knew they weren't. Yet when he looked in her eyes as they talked, he had great hopes.

He'd heard her slip so often lately. She'd mentioned blessings and yesterday she'd quoted scripture. If that wasn't a sign from God, he didn't know what was. She'd left a crack in her armor and the Holy Spirit knew where to sneak in.

His pulse quickened when he gazed at Rona beside him in the SUV as they headed for First Christian Church. He hoped she'd see the kindness of the pastor or even like the attractive building, anything to get her to attend. Even once would open her heart more, he felt confident.

The silence settled around them. Rona had drifted into her own thoughts, and he, in his. He loved the way they could laugh and talk, then settle easily into the quiet of their own thinking.

He'd so longed to know more about Rona. She'd given him that bitter summary of her family. He knew she'd loved her mother and guessed she'd wanted to love her father and brother, but alcohol and who knows what else had kept her from doing that.

Her brother caused him the most concern. He guessed Rona had come to Hessel to escape him more than find herself, and he wanted to know why. She'd avoided talking about family until he pushed, but he understood. He'd told her little about Jill and his recent talks with Gary. If he truly cared about Rona, he should be open with her. He needed someone to talk with and he'd already thought that maybe God had sent Rona into his life as a release from his solitude in more ways than one.

When he glanced toward her again, she looked back at him. "We're both quiet today."

"It's nice, isn't it?"

She gave him a tender smile. "Sometimes it is, but I've had a lot of quiet time to think. Sometimes I like a little excitement."

Excitement? "Then you're sure to love the Thornton home." He sent her an I-hope-you-understand look.

She nodded. "I haven't gotten the total picture yet."

He felt a prayer leave him, asking God to spare her the worst of it. "Maybe Gary will change after this incident. I'm hoping a job and getting back to his friends at church might make a difference. He seemed to fit in so well until he pulled away."

"People pull away to punish themselves sometimes. Other times it's a cry for help. Maybe Gary has something he needs to talk about, something he wants to get off his chest."

"I've sensed that." Gary had talked about Jill, but what else bothered him? Nick longed to find out and soon.

He turned into the church parking lot, pleased to see the number of youth volunteers giving the grounds a spring cleaning. When he saw Pastor Al, Nick gave him a wave, parked and motioned Rona to join him. Though she hesitated, he saw her push open the door and follow.

"How's it going?" he asked as he came closer.

"Great." The Pastor swung his arm, pointing in every direction. "We have kids all over the place."

"Pastor, this is Rona Meyers. She's…a friend and our new housekeeper."

"Nice to meet you, Rona. Are you new in town?"

She nodded and Nick noted that she looked uncomfortable.

"We'd love to see you join us tomorrow for worship."

Rona hesitated, as if trying to find words. "Thank you," she said finally.

Nick jumped in. "Have you seen Ga—"

"Last I saw Gary he was around the corner digging up the flower beds." He gave Nick a wink.

"Thanks." Nick wasn't sure what the wink meant. He reached for a handshake, then patted the pastor's shoulder instead when Pastor Al held up his dirt-laden fingers.

He gave Rona a nod to follow and she moved into step with him. When they rounded the corner, Nick understood the wink.

Gary had collected a bevy of girls who were planting flowers while he dug up the beds.

He gave Rona an arched brow and she grinned. "Should I ask? Is this like father, like son?"

"Not me," Nick said, hoping to sound lighthearted and giving Gary a call.

His son spun around, a startled look on his face that quickly turned to a frown. "What's up?"

"I thought you might want a ride to work." Nick saw the girls' attention turn their way.

Gary glanced at his watch. "I still have an hour. It only takes a few minutes to get there." He lowered his voice. "I want to get the volunteer hours over with."

Disappointed, Nick stood a minute without speaking. "Okay. We came to town to do a few things and I thought I'd offer."

"Jeanie offered to drive me to work." Gary gestured toward one of the prettiest girls in the bunch.

Nick nodded and sent up a prayer. "Okay. Just don't be late on your first day."

Gary scowled. "I won't, Dad."

Nick backed away with Rona at his side. When they were out of view, he stopped and shook his head. "I'm hoping he'll want to get more involved here when his volunteer hours are over. I'm praying for it."

Rona touched his arm. "It would be good for him. He's doing a pretty good job of making friends."

Her comment made him laugh. "Or enemies depending on who's looking at it. Some of those guys might be envious."

"Church boys envious? That's a sin."

Nick chuckled and clasped her arm. Rona's faith

had begun to grow. *Thank You, Lord.* That would be one worry off his mind and give him time to concentrate on his son.

We'd love to see you join us tomorrow for worship. Rona didn't know if she should laugh or cry. God wouldn't give up and she'd gotten to the point that fighting Him seemed ridiculous. Nick's faith powered him in his darkest hours. He'd been strong during Gary's latest situation—upset, yes, but never wavering. He's proven a wonderful example of what faith should do. Maybe the Lord hadn't failed her, but she had failed the Lord.

She liked the pastor's friendly manner. He'd looked delighted when talking about the number of youth working to spruce up the church grounds and his voice sounded caring and his smile seemed kind.

When she dropped the church-issue from her thoughts, she looked at the highway, surprised they were heading toward Cedarville. They'd passed her old motel, bringing back those feelings of loneliness that had been overwhelming when she'd first arrived. Amazing how three weeks could make such a difference.

She looked at Nick's handsome profile. "Why are we going to Cedarville?"

"I thought I'd show you something interesting, something I don't think you know about the islands."

Rona looked out the passenger window, desiring to ask questions but not wanting to ruin his surprise. Nick seemed to delight in doing thoughtful things for her. He'd cleaned the apartment, cooked her a glorious meal on Memorial Day—so many little things that made her feel special.

The trees flashed past and in a little distance, he turned onto Hill Road—she noticed on the sign—and when they crossed a short bridge, he stopped and pointed.

"Hill Island."

Rona turned to look at him. "We're on one of the islands?"

"A couple are connected with bridges." He pulled away, grinning as if he had another surprise for her. He followed the narrow road, turned right and crossed another bridge, then pulled to the shoulder. "Let's get out. It's a nice view."

Rona looked ahead toward the backdrop of dark evergreens to a sea-green sign with Island 8 painted in bright gold letters within a scroll design. "Number eight. Isn't that a strange name for an island?"

Nick shrugged. "Maybe they ran out of names."

She smiled at his comment and followed him outside. He ambled to the guardrail and pointed to the boat docks built with boxlike structures beneath them. To help them last in the freezing weather, he told her. Ahead she saw boathouses and docks with speedboats and runabouts moored to their side; she guessed the houses were deeper in the woods.

The blue sky and the quiet put her at rest. She turned to face the other view and felt drawn to the landscape. "It's so awesome."

Rona crossed the road and leaned against the rail, looking out at a small pontoon boat at the end of a long dock adorned with an American flag. The boat was surrounded by tall grasses jutting up from the lake with only a narrow path leading to the clear water. She'd felt hemmed in like that so often, but sometimes the path out of her dilemma wasn't as obvious as the one she saw today.

Nick stood close beside her. She felt his arm brush against hers softly.

"Look at the view," he whispered.

She looked out beyond the circular tree-lined bank and admired the islands dotting the silver-blue water. "It's peaceful."

Nick turned his back from the scene and rested it against the guardrail. "I wish my mind felt this tranquil."

Rona caught an inflection in his voice that spoke to her. He wanted to talk. "Tell me about it."

His brow lifted as if astounded she'd understood. He bent and pulled a blade of tall grass from along the fence and ran his fingernail along its vein. "It's confusing and I'm not sure what is the truth and what isn't."

She listened as he began telling her about his wife and Gary's comments. "I never thought about it before, but when I think back, I realize now she was unhappy. Maybe it was my work hours. Maybe it was Marquette Island. I'd moved into the house for her. I could have sold it after my parents died. Jill sometimes talked about feeling stranded, even though she had the runabout."

He shrugged and Rona saw the pain in his eyes.

"I'd always thought maybe the accident had been my fault. I hadn't noticed the raft. I hadn't been there before that I can remember, but I'd turned back to look at her, and the next thing I know, she'd swung out and smacked into it. She'd died so fast, and—"

Tears welled in his eyes. "And Gary saw it. He was thirteen and saw everything. I know he blames me."

She'd known. Rona didn't speak but lifted her arms and wrapped them around his torso. Nick lowered his head to her hair and she could feel his body quaking beneath her hands. Gary had hurt him to the core with his attack, but if Nick had been careless, it had still been an accident. The facts spun in her mind.

"I'm sorry," he said, lifting his head.

She looked into his glassy eyes and felt her own tears well. "Nick, it was an accident."

He blinked and shook his head. "I'm not sure now. If Jill had been drinking, then something serious had been wrong. I never understood how she'd hit the raft. She'd been a good skier."

She realized he'd deduced something new from what Gary had said and she feared she understood what he was saying.

"I'm afraid Jill ran into the raft on purpose."

Suicide? The word struck Rona like a knife.

"Her judgment might have been impaired. It could have been anything."

He stayed silent a moment. "You're right. I don't suppose we'll ever know." He swallowed and raised his eyes toward the islands in the distance. "But Gary blames me, and I have no explanation for what happened."

"You do," she said, lifting her hand and pressing it against his cheek. "I understand. You don't want to add to Gary's worry."

"How can I tell him that Jill may have taken her own life?"

She drew her fingers along his strong jaw, feeling

the beginning raspiness of whiskers. "And maybe she didn't, so you can't tell him that."

He nodded and lifted his right hand to press against hers. "I suppose. What good would it do anyway?"

"And Gary's problem could be deeper than he's saying. He might be sorry that he didn't tell you about the wine. He might be…anything. You don't know how much blame he's put on himself."

"That crossed my mind, too. If things calm down and Gary becomes more like the son I had before Jill died, I hope we can talk."

"You will," she whispered.

Their gaze connected and Rona's chest tightened with the look in his eyes. She knew what could happen at any moment, and though part of her wanted to step away, the other part drew closer.

Nick's eyes searched hers and she couldn't hide the longing she felt any more than she could push him away. His arms pulled her to him and his mouth lowered to hers with a kiss so gentle, yet so demanding, she couldn't breathe.

When he drew back, his face filled with apology. "I shouldn't have—"

She pressed her finger against his lips. "Should haves are in the past. Now is important."

He pulled her into his arms and kissed her again.

Nick had struggled with himself since he'd kissed Rona on the Island 8 bridge. Every minute had thrilled him, but when his logic had returned, he realized he'd gone against his own wisdom.

Though Rona had shown him more and more that

she'd only been angry at the Lord and not that she'd been an unbeliever, he needed to be assured before he could allow himself to fall in love with her. The idea sent him spinning. Too late. He'd already fallen and hard. But he sensed she had concerns, too, and to form a bond blessed by God, they both needed to be certain about a lot of things. He couldn't go on kissing her this way without moving deeper into a relationship, and he knew that wouldn't be God-pleasing.

His chest clinched. Why had these wild sensations happened in the first place? He'd only wanted a house-keeper. Voices in the house. Food on the stove. Not these intense feelings.

After dinner, Gary had gone to his room, complaining about a sore back and aching arms, and Rona had gone out back. He'd sent her away with the insistence that he'd load the dishwasher. After he'd wiped off the table and poured a final cup of coffee, he walked to the breakfast nook and looked outside.

Nick watched her for a moment and studied her petite figure, the shape of her shoulders appearing when her long strands of shining hair shifted in the breeze. He gazed, amazed for once to be filled with joy and wonder.

He closed his eyes, wishing the vision would vanish because he wasn't able to pursue anything yet. Rona gave him hope when his hope had been so dim and re-membrance when he'd wanted to have nothing to do with memories. All they could do was cloud his judg-ment.

He'd often complimented Rona on her wise judg-ment, and he felt certain hers was stronger than his. He couldn't deal with rejection and he feared that's what he would get from Rona even though he knew she cared about him.

He'd known once what it had been like to hold a woman in his arms and to love her as only a married couple could. Rona caused him to long to be a family again, to have a wife and a son who smiled. He recalled the good times with Jill, memories for once untainted by sorrow. Recollection that sent new possibilities into his mind.

Reeling with thoughts, he opened the sliding door to the patio and stepped outside. Rona had settled at the end of the picnic table where the sunlight lingered the longest. As he approached, she glanced over her shoulder and smiled.

Nick pushed aside his pondering and settled beside her on the bench, sipping his coffee and listening to the muted sounds from the lake, the caw of a bird and the beating of his heart.

"Are you okay?" she asked, breaking the silence.

He slipped his hand over hers and brushed his fingers across her skin. "I'm fine. Kitchen's clean."

She chuckled. "Thanks for the break. Any sounds from Gary?"

"No. I can hear the thud of bass on his CD player but that's about it."

She shifted to face him. "You've seemed concerned all evening. If it's the kiss, I'm as guilty as you are and I know it meant nothing. It came out of the emotion of the moment."

Meant nothing. His heart screamed. Yet how could he respond?

"I didn't stop you, Nick. I could have, but I didn't."

"It meant something, don't say it didn't. And, yes it came out of emotion—feelings I have for you, but I need to respect you. You keep reminding me we've only known each other for a short time. To me it's a lifetime."

She released a sigh. "Me, too."

They fell quiet again, but inside he was far from quiet. He felt the Lord prodding him, pushing him. He resisted until he couldn't any longer.

"Did you like Pastor Al?"

She turned her gaze to his. "I don't know him, but he seems nice. Very caring and kind."

"He is." His feet shuffled beneath the bench, fighting the words on his lips.

She tilted her head, her face tender with understanding. "You want to ask me to go to church with you."

"How did you know?"

She lifted her shoulders. "I've sensed it as a problem."

"Is it a problem, Rona? I'd hoped—"

She ran her fingers through her hair, pushing it from her face. "The Lord has been driving me up a wall lately."

He felt his eyes widen. "What?"

"I fought God for so long and I give up." She lifted her hands heavenward. "He wins."

Her look melted his heart. "He wins?"

"I'll go to church with you tomorrow."

He heard resignation in her voice, but that didn't matter. The Holy Spirit had His way and when He was determined, He succeeded. "That makes me so happy."

"I'm relieved." She shook her head. "You've been an amazing example to me and I realized the other day that God didn't fail me as much as I failed Him."

He wove his fingers through hers. "You can say God won, Rona, but you know what?"

She lifted her brows.

"You won even more. Repentance is a beautiful thing. So are you." He looked over his shoulder. "I'd love to kiss you right now, but Gary might be watching."

Rona slipped her fingers from his. "Then we'd better be careful with this, too, don't you think?"

He didn't want to stop, but once again, Rona's wise thinking won out.

Chapter Twelve

Monday afternoon, Rona folded laundry while the praise music from yesterday's service filled her head. When she first walked through the church doors, she felt like a stranger, but once she'd settled into her seat, listened to the voices lifting in song, heard the prayers and the Word of God, she felt as if she'd just opened a box that she'd put away for years and found a wonderful gift inside.

How could so many months—years—of anger at God dissipate as swiftly as the morning dew? Yet what hadn't left her was the sense of being a sinner. She'd turned her back on God and He'd clung to her with His strong cord, allowing her to make stupid decisions and to rail Him for what He hadn't done for her while she did nothing for Him.

Nick had gazed at her numerous times during the service, hoping, she knew, that she would open her heart.

Today she could still hear their conversation from their trip home from church.

"How did it go?"

"Good," she'd said. "It's like coming home. Sort of the prodigal son returning to his father, except I returned to my heavenly Father, but I still have a price to pay. I'm such a sinner."

He had slipped his hand over hers. "Rona, we're all sinners. Every one of us. Didn't you listen to the readings?"

She told him she had. Still, the readings hadn't referred to her sins. Her sins seemed far worse than those of the everyday Christian. She'd been gone too long.

"You heard the verse in Psalms. You are blessed because you have not lied, but told God the truth about your sin. You've repented and God doesn't count your sins against you. You are sinless in His sight."

Though he made sense and she had heard Pastor Al's reading, she had one major problem. "I guess I'm not sinless in my own eyes."

"Forgive yourself, Rona. Hand over the burden. Jesus has offered to carry it." He released the steering wheel with one hand and nestled her shoulder against his. "It takes time. Don't chastise yourself."

The words echoed in her memory as she folded the last pair of jeans and laid them on the pile. She drew in a breath. Nick was right, and from now on she needed to cling to the Lord rather than push Him away.

She grinned to herself. It hadn't done any good trying to break loose before. The Holy Spirit had a hold on her and hadn't planned to let go. "Thank You, Lord," she whispered.

Hoisting the pile of laundry, Rona headed to the staircase. She'd heard Gary arrive when she was eating lunch in her apartment. He hadn't shown his face since and she wondered if he'd eaten.

Rona stopped in Nick's bedroom and dropped off what she hoped were his clothes. Gary was more slender, so she calculated she had sorted them right. Then she took the stairs to the second floor and stopped outside Gary's door.

Inside, she thought she heard voices. A radio, maybe. She waited a minute before tapping on the door. "Gary, I have your laundry."

A scuffle noise came from inside.

"Gary?" Her heart thumped with concern. "Are you alright?"

"Leave it outside." His muffled voice came through the door.

With her pulse racing, she tried to make sense out of what she heard. "Open the door. I'm not putting clean clothes on the floor."

More noise and shuffling.

"Gary. Please open the door."

Finally the door inched open, and he reached out for the laundry, but before Gary could shut the door again, Rona caught her breath, her heart sinking. A pair of women's shoes laid at the side of his bed.

She grasped the knob. "You have someone in there."

His look stabbed her. "It's none of your business."

She felt a shudder down her back. "I'm sorry, but it is. I'm in charge when your father's not here. In fact, he's going to be late tonight so you're stuck with me all evening."

"Great." Daggers shot from his eyes.

Rona studied the feminine shoes. "Amy?"

With her hair disheveled and her clothes in disarray, Amy stepped from behind the door, her face the color of mottled pink fabric.

"Amy, you and Gary will have to leave the room."

Gary shifted her aside and strode in front of her. "This is my room, and I can do—"

"Gary, you owe your father the respect to behave in the house he shares with you. He loves you and he's asked me to take over when he's gone. I'm just doing my job."

"Loves me? I don't think so."

"He loves you, but you'll have to learn that for yourself—if you give him a chance."

He dug his fists into his pockets. "I suppose you'll be on the phone in two minutes to report in."

Her chest tightened with her flash decision. "I'll tell you what. I've known about your smoking for a while and I haven't said a word, because I hoped it would stop. I'm not going to say anything now if you go downstairs. You're welcome to go outside. I'll make you lunch. But if I get lip from you, I'll have to tell him."

He studied her a moment, his brow knit so tight his eyes were slits. "You won't say anything? Why?"

"Because I believe in forgiveness." The words struck her cold. She'd been unforgiving so many times in her life, unforgiving of her father and her brother. Could she ever forgive Don?

"I don't get you." He tilted his head while Amy clung to him, clutching the top of her blouse that had been partially unbuttoned.

"I don't get me, either, but I like your dad. I think you've both struggled with the past far too long."

His eyebrows raised. "What do you know about my past?"

Why had she mentioned it? A knot twisted in her throat. "Enough. We'll talk about it another time." She gestured toward the stairs. "Why don't you pick up your shoes, Amy, and both of you go downstairs."

Amy peered at her bare feet and her shoes beside the bed, realizing the telltale evidence that had given her away. She snatched her shoes and fled past Rona toward the staircase.

Rona kept her eyes focused on Gary. "What do you say?"

"Fine," he said, dropping his laundry on the end of the bed, then straightening his knit shirt and strutting past her.

Rona stood a moment, overwhelmed by what had happened. She'd promised not to tell Nick and now she felt it had been a mistake. She didn't want to be a patsy for Gary. He needed to know she wasn't going to tolerate bad behavior just to protect him from his father, but she wanted so badly for their relationship to be repaired. They both had love to give and that's what she wanted to see.

She closed her eyes. *You can do it, Lord.* A strange release rolled over her as she turned toward the staircase.

Nick looked at the sun overhead, grateful he'd decided to take a break from his busy schedule. He missed spending time at home and he had concerns about Rona. She looked stressed and though she hadn't made any comments about Gary, he wondered.

He steered the boat past Long Island, watching his boathouse grow larger as he closed the distance. He wanted to do something special tonight or if not tonight, then soon. Rona had worked hard and though he'd told her to take her days off, she had nothing to do and stayed at the house, always making dinner or surprising him with baked goods.

He patted his paunch, knowing he'd have to watch the calories if Rona insisted on plying him with sweets. Sweets. Her sweetness nuzzled against his heart. He'd longed to kiss her again, but he'd stopped himself, fearing Gary would see and not understand or he'd frighten Rona by moving too fast.

His spirit had soared since she'd agreed to go to church and, though he saw no difference in her behavior—she'd always been a Christian at heart—he felt the strain had lifted. She seemed happier, except for those dark moments that clouded her eyes. He'd avoided asking. He had a bad habit of pushing too hard.

The warm wind sneaked into the boat cabin and the warm sun beat against his arms. They could go swimming or picnic on Government Island. Something. He hadn't done enough with Gary, though he'd noticed a different look in his eyes. His son had studied him at times, as if trying to figure him out or to find the courage to talk. Nick didn't know which. No matter. He prayed it was an improvement.

He nosed the boat between the docks, tied it, then picked up the bouquet of flowers he'd purchased and headed inside. When Nick opened the door, he smelled the clean scent and knew Rona had been at work.

Nick strode through the foyer, veered past the family room and glanced into the kitchen. Disappointed that Rona wasn't there, he lay the flowers on the kitchen counter and retraced his steps to enter his bedroom.

When he stepped into the room's sitting area, he saw another stack of laundry on the end of his neatly made bed. Rona. His heart sang with the joy of her in the house. She brought sunshine and life. He slipped out of his clothes, stepped into walking shorts and pulled on a polo shirt.

After he tucked his feet into a pair of moccasins, he returned to the kitchen, found a large pitcher and filled it with water. He had no idea where a vase was, but this would do. He settled the flowers into the pitcher and set it on the table in the breakfast nook. When he pulled back, he saw Rona in the backyard.

An unexpected jolt of happiness shot through him, and he slid open the French door and stepped onto the patio. When he slid it closed, she looked up.

"What are you doing home?" She rose from her knees, a trowel in her hand, and waited.

Nick saw the trays of flowers at her feet, then realized she'd planted them around the patio and had another bed in a sunny spot not too far from the picnic table. "Looks great. Where did you get those?"

She grinned. "In town. I wanted to surprise you."

And she had. He compared his single bouquet sitting inside with the live flowers she'd purchased and planted. "What can I say?"

"Nothing." She stepped toward him. "It's nice to see you."

Her smile made him weak. What could he do? He glanced back at the house. "Is Gary home yet?"

"No. He got a call from the pastor this morning. The

youth are doing yard work at senior citizens' houses today, so he agreed to go until he goes to work. He's on the late shift."

His joy shrank, realizing Rona knew more about Gary than he did. "Are you two getting along?"

"We have an understanding."

He wondered what that meant, but again, he let it drop. "Can I help?" He motioned to the flowers.

"No, I'm nearly finished and you're in clean clothes."

He glanced at the shorts, realizing she'd just washed them. "Then I'll bring you out a ginger ale. How's that?"

She nodded and he headed inside, trying to decide what he could do to say thank-you. He grabbed two drinks from the refrigerator and a bag of potato chips, then returned to the yard and sat on the picnic bench and watched her.

The sunlight still brightened the yard and shined on Rona's hair like a flame, highlighting her honey-colored waves with flashes of pale copper. She'd tanned the past week and her skin looked healthy and glowing. He managed to stay on the bench and not pull her into his arms.

Finally Rona set the trowel in the plastic tray along with her garden gloves, which had a flowery design. She ambled to his side. "Thanks for the drink." She settled on the bench and gazed at her handiwork.

"It looks nice. Thanks so much."

She gave him a crooked smile. "I thought it was about time the place had a woman's touch."

His heart burst with longing. He needed a woman's influence. Though he wanted to speak, to tell her so much, he managed to hold it in. It was better that way.

She swallowed a long drink of the ginger ale, then set down the can and swiveled toward him. "How long have you lived on Marquette?"

"About nine years, since my dad died. I lived in a smaller place on Drummond."

She tilted her head and her hair brushed across her shoulder, leaving him speechless again. "And now you own both."

It wasn't a question, but he nodded and gained his senses. "Marquette is difficult in the winter. My parents usually went to Arizona when the ice began to freeze. They had a condo near Tucson."

Her back straightened. "I was thinking about that today. What do you do in the winter?"

"We live on Drummond. They keep the ferry running in the winter. It just makes Gary's school more difficult. You know, a longer ride."

A frown settled again on her face. "What happens to me when you move back?"

"I have a comfortable cabin there, too. Angie liked it."

"Angie?" Surprise filled her eyes followed by a frown.

"My previous housekeeper."

Her scowl lessened. "She quit?"

"Moved. To St. Ignace."

She looked back toward the trays and Nick knew she was ready to clean up the gardening mess. Rona didn't leave things undone. He'd learned that quickly enough. Just like a wife. Wife. The word fluttered in his chest. "Would you like to see the house and cabin?"

Her brow knit again. "You mean on Drummond?"

"Sure. Why not? It's early. We'll stop for dinner in Cedarville on the way back. Ang-Gio's has great food."

She studied him a moment, then stood up.

He grinned, realizing the word *cabin* sounded very rustic. She'd be surprised when she saw it.

"I'd love to see the cabin and the house, too."

Nick darted ahead of her and stacked the flower trays before she could, then handed her the trowel and gloves. He emptied the trash into the bin while she carried the trowel and gloves inside. He hurried to catch her.

"Nick." She spun round as he came through the door. "They're beautiful." Her eyes sparkled. "Especially the vase." She lifted the pitcher in her hand and gazed at the flowers. "I love fresh flowers in the house."

"You've spent the whole day filling the yard with them and I bring you a paltry bouquet."

She set down the pitcher and faced him with the tenderest look he'd ever scene. "No one has ever given me flowers before."

He stood in front of her with his mouth gaping. "No one?"

She bit her lip and shook her head. "Thank you."

He stepped forward and put his hands on her shoulders. "They're for the apartment."

"No. We'll leave them here. This is where I spend so much time. Let me get ready and I'll find a vase later." Before she moved, she took a step closer, tiptoed, and gave him the sweetest kiss he'd ever known.

Chapter Thirteen

❧

On the trip to Drummond Island, Nick had quizzed her about Gary. The more they talked the more guilty she'd become. She'd promised Gary and she couldn't break that promise without doing damage to their relationship. He'd stopped being mouthy and even helped her a few times when she needed a strong back.

Nick shifted his back. "Bernie said Gary's doing well—working hard and arriving on time. I guess I can stop worrying about that."

"I talked with Mandy. She said the same thing. He's a little quiet, she said, but that's better than being mouthy."

Nick gave a giant nod in agreement. "How's he with you?"

The question made her tense. "Pretty good. He's been helpful at times. Messy at others, but that's a teenager. It goes with the territory."

He released a sigh. "I'm feeling guilty about Gary."

Rona shifted to face him. "Why?"

He shrugged. "I'm working long hours and not seeing him, and he's done a good job. He's working and turning over his money with only some grumbling. Naturally, I give him some spending money."

His comment reminded her of the soft side of Nick's nature.

"And he's nearly finished his volunteer hours. My work is under control, for now, anyway, and I want to do something with Gary. I thought maybe we could go to Government Island for a picnic and swimming."

Government Island. She managed not to frown. "It sounds like a prison. You know, like Alcatraz Island."

Nick chuckled. "It's an uninhabited island just off La Salle Island and part of the Hiawatha National Forest. It's a fun day trip."

"Gary would probably like that." She hoped he would, at least. "I noticed you have that big extra room upstairs. That could make a nice—"

"Game room."

He'd read her mind.

"I've been thinking about that. Maybe buy a foosball or pool table, something fun and something he and I could do, and he could bring home friends." He shrugged. "I'm not sure that will happen, though."

"Don't give up before you try it." She gave his arm a nudge. "I think it's a good idea."

He sent her a fleeting grin before they settled into silence, her mind going over her trials with Gary. Although she'd noticed some positive changes; she feared they were due to the threat she had hanging over Gary's head.

When they boarded the ferry, Rona thought of her

unexpected meeting with Nick at the Four Corners information center. Nick's comments on soul mates had also struck her and she'd begun to wonder if meeting him that day had been coincidental or part of God's doing. The Lord had been guiding her all along and she'd never realized it.

In the quiet of the SUV, Nick leaned back and slipped his hand over hers, caressing her fingers like a summer breeze. Neither spoke. She felt no need to and apparently he didn't, either.

The short trip ended and Nick started the motor, ready to move over the ramp to the island. He talked about the limestone quarry and the days of his ancestors' logging business and before she knew it, they had passed through Four Corners and were heading along Johnswood Road. Rona had no idea what to expect and the farther they drove the more curious she became.

"How large is this house?"

"It's much smaller—living room, dining room, kitchen, three bedrooms and two baths. The kitchen has a breakfast nook and a laundry room off of it. Small but nice."

Small but nice. It sounded like a mansion to Rona.

"The cabin is smaller yet, but I think you'll like it."

When Nick slowed she spotted a stone house nestled in a wooded area heavy with large trees and thick with evergreens.

"Here we are."

She felt her jaw drop. "It's not what I expected."

He looked at her with a question on his face.

"It's so interesting with the stone and logs."

He opened the door. "It's smaller than the other house, so less work for you."

She followed him to the long covered porch and waited while he unlocked the door. Inside, the house smelled unused, but she knew that a few days of open windows or, in winter, a warm fire would take away the scent. She stood in the foyer and looked ahead to a large living room that ended with a huge stone fireplace. On each side she saw French doors.

"Nick, it's gorgeous." She pointed to the fireplace and hurried to admire it more closely, her palm running over the heavy fieldstone. When she peeked through a side door, another large porch greeted her and beyond that a wooded landscape. Her heart stood still when she saw the cabin nestled among the trees, a large stone chimney rising above the roof.

"Nick!" She couldn't control the yell. "It's wonderful. Can we go see?" She felt like a child standing in front of the Christmas tree and waiting to open her gifts.

He hurried to her side and slipped his arm around her waist. "That's what we're here for."

Nick took her hand and led her through the yard to the cabin. A small covered slab led to the door and when they stepped inside she stood in a small foyer beside the stone fireplace at the end of a huge living room. The furniture was cozy with rag rugs and warm colors.

At the far end of the room, she turned and entered a kitchen larger than the one in her apartment with a table and chairs. Two bedrooms were situated on the other side of the house and to her delight, a flagstone-covered patio opened off the living room.

"I told you you'd love it." He opened his arms to her and she stepped into his embrace.

She felt his lips press against her hair and her heart soared until reality set her straight. Nick liked her. He said they were soul mates and she felt the same, but she didn't fit into his world. She'd never met his friends, knew nothing of his social circle except that they had no place for a woman with no breeding and no money.

"What's wrong?" He drew back and looked into her face.

"This feels too good to be true."

"It's all true, Rona. It's—" He faltered, then took her hand. "Let's go back to the house. It's not as damp."

She hadn't even noticed the dampness until he mentioned it. The cabin needed love. So did she.

Rona followed Nick inside the main house and he motioned to the sofa in front of the fireplace.

"I'll start a fire and get out some of the mustiness."

The beautiful June day hardly seemed time for a fire, but Rona agreed that the house did feel damp after being closed up so much since he'd moved over to Marquette Island.

"Do you have anything to drink?" she asked before sitting.

"Pop maybe. It's probably out of date. You should find tea over the cabinet above the coffeemaker." She headed into the kitchen, slipped a teakettle onto the burner and located tea bags. By the time she returned with two mugs, flames danced in the fireplace.

She handed Nick a mug and settled onto the sofa,

enjoying the warmth of the fire. She took at sip of her drink and set it on the coffee table in front of her.

Nick settled beside her, his mug cupped between his hands.

Silence settled around them again, but Rona sensed that Nick had something to say. The easy quiet she usually felt, today, seemed charged with questions.

She heard Nick release a deep breath. "Rona, do you know how I feel about you?"

She pondered, wanting to be honest but not knowing what the truth was. She'd sensed he had strong feelings for her. The kisses and embraces confirmed that, but it didn't fit. She tossed it off as gratitude and then as wishful thinking. A man who'd experienced marriage needed to test the waters to learn if he could play the romance game again and she might be his trial run. Her chest constricted as she struggled with her thoughts.

"You must know," he whispered. "I care about you so much. Not as a housekeeper, but as a woman who's awakened me to the emptiness I've been living and to the dream of being a family again."

Time stood still as she tried to make sense out of what he'd said, knowing if he meant those words she had to tell him the truth about her past.

Rona closed her eyes, drawing on her courage, drawing on the faith she'd just come to know again. God said He would be with her in times of trouble and the truth roared in her ears. "I think more of you than I can say. You've been like a dream come true to me, but you don't know everything about me, Nick."

He grasped her hands. "Then tell me and I'll understand."

It sounded so easy. "I don't fit into your world. I was raised by a poor family, a father who drank most of the money he earned, a mother who tried so hard to raise us well."

Nick pressed his palm against hers. "And she did."

"She tried, but she failed. I haven't told you about my brother." She swallowed, trying to keep her voice calm, trying to quell the images. "He's been in prison and he was supposed to be released in May. He might be out now. It was a robbery, but not his first. He's been in trouble since I can remember."

"But you told me yourself. The sins of the father aren't the sins of the son. That works for a sister, too. You're not to blame for your brother's crimes."

A weight struck her heart as she tried to pull the words from her throat. "I know but—"

"As for not fitting into my world, you fit like a glove. You haven't had a chance to know my friends. They'll love you." His free hand shifted to caress her cheek. "You're a beautiful woman, but what means most to me is your strength and depth. Your energy and determination."

She lowered her head as tension mounted. "But you don't know about my bitterness."

He tilted her head upward and looked into her eyes. "I heard resentment in your voice when you first told me about your family. I've been bitter, too, Rona, bitter at Jill for dying, bitter at Gary for withdrawing, bitter at myself for not making my marriage a better one."

"Since I've been doing so much soul-searching, I really need to resolve some issues at home. I don't know if I can, but I'm trying to deal with it. I'm praying that God gives me what I need to let it go."

Nick drew her into his arms, his voice whispering against her cheek. "We both have some praying and soul-searching to do, but don't toss out what we have. I hope you believe me when I tell you that you've opened doors and windows for me and I'm not letting go of you."

She clung to him, not wanting to let go, but so afraid of hanging on.

"Where's my dad?"

Rona jumped and nearly dropped the salad, hearing Gary's voice. "He's getting the boat ready."

She looked over her shoulder. "Where's Amy?"

He motioned toward the French door. "She's in the backyard."

Rona slipped the bread on top of the other items and closed the basket lid, then turned to face Gary. "Is something wrong?"

He shrugged. "She's moody. I shouldn't have invited her to come along."

That surprised her. Her mind clicked with possibilities. Gary had seemed different and she'd been so pleased when Nick had finally acted on his idea from a week ago to do something special with Gary. Today was the day, but now she wasn't sure if things would go right or not.

She glanced toward Gary again, deciding he had a concern on his mind. "Can I help you with something?"

"Are you going to the island with us?"

She had to juggle that question. "Yes, unless you'd rather I didn't."

"I don't care one way or the other."

Rona took that as a positive. "I've never been there."

Silence slipped between them again.

She picked up the basket. "Will you carry this out to your dad?"

Gary leaned against the counter. "I stopped smoking."

He'd looked away, and she couldn't see his face. "I'm glad. You love sports and I think you'll have more energy."

Gary bit the edge of his fingernail as if thinking. "So what did my dad tell you about me?"

His uneasiness confused her. "I didn't tell your dad anything, Gary. I promised I wouldn't. I hope one day you'll tell him yourself."

"That's not what I meant. What did my dad tell you about me? He told you about my past, remember?"

She drew up her shoulders, thinking it was a bad time to get into this, but she had little choice. "I know you saw your mother's accident and it's been hard on you."

He studied her face, as if trying to dig deeper. "What else?"

"Your dad said you'd seen her drinking. That surprised him." She turned away unable to keep thoughts straight with his probing look.

"That's because he was never home."

Her head lashed in his direction. "Never?"

Gary gave a tilt of his head. "Seemed that way. Just like now. He worked long hours."

"I know. He does it to give you a good home." She

swung her arm toward the rest of the house. "Two good homes. I never knew such luxury until I came here to work."

He screwed up his face in disbelief. "What do you mean?"

"I was poor. My dad was an alcoholic who spent most of our money so we had to struggle for the things we needed. My mom had a hard time. She died before I was married."

"You're married?"

She shook her head. "My husband died. He was a drunk, too."

His expression filled with a question. "You're just saying this."

Rona raised her hand. "Scout's honor." Then wondering if he knew what that meant, she added, "Really. It was a bad life. That's what makes me sad when I see you and your dad so distant. You both deserve better."

Gary glanced outside without saying anything. "I'd better go out and—" he swung his hand toward the doorway "—and get Amy."

"Will you take the basket?"

"I'll be back." He opened the door. "Can you pick me up tomorrow night? Dad said he's going to some kind of meeting on the island."

"Sure. What's happening tomorrow?"

"The church is having a party for the youth volunteers. Pizza and stuff. I figured I might as well go."

Hearing that, Rona's pulse jogged. "I'd be happy to."

"I'm going to ask Dad if I can spend the night with Randy. He can drop me off at work in the morning."

Church. Randy. He'd given her so much information, especially about his feelings. "Check with your dad."

He nodded and stepped outside.

Rona held her breath, praying this was something good happening. Nick may have been right. Getting into trouble, then getting back with his old friends at church may have been one of God's blessings.

Now that she thought about it, her trouble had brought her here, too. Maybe God had planned for her to meet Nick so He could give her an unbelievable blessing.

Chapter Fourteen

"**G**reat lunch," Nick said, pushing away his plate. He eyed Gary, noticing he hadn't scarfed down his food as usual and that Amy had only picked at hers. "Aren't you two going swimming?"

Although he'd planned this picnic for his son, Gary seemed to be in a dreamworld. Gary loved to swim, and his reticence concerned Nick. After a moment, Nick asked again, trying to understand what was going on.

Gary eyed Amy. "Are you gonna swim?"

Amy gave a vague shrug and looked away, while Nick tried to figure out what was going on.

Gary swung his legs over the bench, focusing on Amy. "I'm gonna run for a few minutes. If you decide you want to swim, let me know." He pulled his T-shirt over his head and dropped it on the bench.

As Gary darted off, Nick opened his mouth, ready to warn him about eating and swimming, but Gary had eaten so little that it probably didn't matter. Anyway, he remembered reading somewhere that doctors now thought eating and swimming was not a problem.

He drew back, wondering what had happened to his attitude. He'd brought Gary here hoping for some family time, but it appeared he'd failed.

He turned to watch Rona packing away the left-overs and putting their paper plates into a trash bag. He strode toward her. "Let me help."

She shook her head. "Why don't you jog along with Gary?"

Since family time had been his motive, he decided to take Rona up on the offer. "I'll be back in a few minutes."

Curious, anyway, he sprinted off, hoping to catch up with Gary, but his youthful son appeared a speck on the long sandy beach. Good exercise, though. If he ran from one end of the long stretch of beach to the other, he'd put in a mile and a half. He drew in a breath and sped after Gary.

"Wait up!"

Gary glanced over his shoulder, then slowed and stopped. He rested his hands on his knees and when Nick arrived, Gary was still panting.

"What's going on?"

Gary tilted his head upward without really look-ing. "Nothing."

Nick gestured toward the picnic tables, then stopped short. He'd been ready to ask about Amy, but he thought better of it. "Ready?"

Gary straightened and trotted off, this time slower. Nick was grateful for that. After a half mile, they stopped, both gasping.

When Nick caught his breath, he rested his hand on

Gary's shoulder. "I want to thank you for finishing the volunteer hours. I'm proud of you for following through."

Although Gary only shrugged, Nick caught the look of surprise on his face. "I know you have a way to go yet with the fine, but—"

"It was my fault, Dad."

This time Nick felt surprised.

Gary looked out toward the water. "You told Rona about Mom."

Nick rocked with the abrupt comment. "I did. I think a lot of Rona, so I'm open with her."

"Did you know her father was a drunk?"

"She told me."

He looked into Nick's eyes. "She was poor."

"She told you that?"

He nodded. "Her mom died, too."

"I know."

Gary turned away. "I think I'll swim back."

"Be careful."

"Dad, I'm not six."

Instead of getting upset, Nick laughed and waved him into the water. He watched Gary for a few moments. He'd grown to be a good swimmer and Nick felt proud, trotting along the beach, trying to keep up with his son and thinking about so many years ago when he was sixteen.

Today Nick realized how well God could heal wounds. Maybe Gary's attitude was a fluke, but maybe not. He'd talked to him for the first time in so long, a real talk without complaints or criticism. It felt good, and what made him feel even better was Rona, who'd shared a little of her life with Gary. Nick had no idea if that had made a difference, but if so, he'd be forever grateful. He sucked in air and shot forward.

Nick pushed open the front door. "Look what I bought," he called into the house.

Rona appeared in the hallway, her eyes narrowing as she scrutinized the box he'd managed to get through the door. "What's that?"

"The foosball table."

"Really?" She ambled closer and eyed the carton. "When did you buy that?"

"I ordered it after we talked." He balanced the box against his leg. "I had them hold it until I knew Gary wasn't home." He chucked her cheek. "Thought I'd surprise you, too."

"You did." She rolled her eyes, yet sent him a smile. "I'll need to get that room cleaned up before anyone gets in there to use it." She stepped closer and rested a hand on the box. "Let me help you boost it upstairs."

"You?" He reached over and gave her biceps a playful squeeze.

Rona flexed her muscles, making him chuckle. "I'll push from the bottom. You can tug."

He nodded, well aware that he needed help getting the awkward box up the staircase. They wrestled the carton upward and at the top, Rona hurried ahead to open the door.

Rona seemed as excited as he hoped Gary would be. She helped him drag the table from the cardboard and set all the legs aside to assemble.

She stood watching him, her hands on her hips.

"You'll need some chairs in here and a table or something."

"How about a card table for now?" He gave her a wink, almost seeing the gears clicking in her mind.

"That'll work, I suppose." She walked closer and rested her hand on his shoulder as he knelt on the floor. "For now."

He motioned toward the far corner. "Look over there. You might find a couple of things."

Rona hurried across the room and lifted the drop cloth. "Here's an old recliner and a lamp table. Great." He watched her pull out another piece from behind the stack. "What kind of table is this?" She pulled open a small drawer on the side.

He studied it. "I think it's an old library table my folks owned."

She brushed her hand over the wood. "We can use it. This is great." She wandered back toward him, her face beaming. "I can't wait to get the room put together."

Nick rose and pulled her into his arms. "You're a good person, Rona. I'm crazy about you." Her eyes glistened into his, making his heart swell. "Gary thinks a lot of you."

"Did he tell you that?"

"I just know, and you get more out of him than I do."

"A woman's touch."

He lifted her hand and pressed it against his cheek. "I like a woman's touch, too."

Rona jerked her hand away, sending him a playful frown. "Gary has been talking more." She glanced away. "And asking questions."

"He mentioned you told him about your family."

"I thought he needed to know that everyone has problems and we survive."

Nick studied her face, knowing she'd more than survived. "Has he said any more about Amy? I know he told you they broke up."

"He did. I guess that's why she had acted so quiet at the picnic. He hadn't said anything to her yet, but she sensed it. He'd told her he wouldn't go with her to something his friends were doing."

"Really?" Nick tossed that idea in the air and mulled it over. "Where's he now? I knew he was going out."

"He worked all day and he's at another church event tonight, something to do with the volunteers."

"He's still doing that even though the community service hours are finished?"

She grinned. "Don't complain."

He slipped his arms around her and drew her closer. "I'm thrilled. I've been watching the change since you've come into our lives and—"

"It has nothing to do with me, Nick." She leaned back to see his face. "You told me you needed to change and I think you have. You've been more positive. I've heard it in your conversation. That's the difference."

"Praise God for the difference," he said, then sent up another thanks for having Rona in his life.

Rona gave him a squeeze and stepped back. "Want to stand this table up?"

He grasped an end while she clasped the other and set the table upright. "I'll have to practice before I tell Gary about it. He'll never find it in here."

Rona's chuckle brightened him. He reached out and took her hand as they left the room and closed the door on the surprise, but when they stood in the hallway, he didn't want to let go.

"I'm excited about this game room. I think it will help my relationship with Gary. I've felt so empty and I'm sure Gary felt that, too. I probably withdrew from him more than I realized. In my heart I wanted to be a family, but without Jill I didn't feel Gary and I were one." He slipped his arm around her shoulder and drew her closer. "I feel differently now."

His lips lowered to hers, yet today he felt a tentative response from Rona until she tensed. He drew away, longing to ask what he'd said or did that made her uncomfortable. Yet reality told him that today she was his housekeeper, not Gary's mother, not his wife, not even his fiancée. He so wanted to see that happen and if it ever would, he needed to act.

He drew his hand along the length of her arm, using the time to organize his thoughts. "I'm going to a benefit dinner next Saturday. It's put on by the DeTour Reef Light Preservation Society to help keep the lighthouse in good repair. It's a wonderful event—Evening Under the Stars." He captured her gaze. "I could use an escort. Would you come with me? It would make me so happy."

Her beautiful mouth tensed and Nick could see her struggling with his request.

"I couldn't, Nick. It's not right."

"What do you mean?"

Her gaze lowered. "I'm your housekeeper and—"

He tilted her chin upward to look in her eyes.

"You're my dearest friend. You mean everything to me. I want you to meet the people I know and—"

She pressed her fingertip against his lips and shook her head. "You'll enjoy yourself without me."

"I won't." His shoulders weighted with her response. "Just think about it, please."

She closed her eyes for a moment, then shook her head again.

Nick felt defeated. If he must, he'd go down fighting, but he wasn't giving up.

Rona drew away. "I had a telephone call today on my cell. I assumed it was you, but it was from my cousin. I gave her the number in case there was an emergency."

"Cousin? Is something wrong?"

"My dad. He's been sick. Sicker than usual. She wanted me to know."

"Why didn't you tell me? You've had this worry on your mind, and I'm bugging you about a dinner."

She waved away his words. "I didn't want to bother you with it."

"It's no bother. Do you want to go home?"

She closed her eyes a moment. "This is home."

His chest tightened.

She focused on him. "But I feel led to do something. I'm going to think about it."

"Don't wait too long. You don't want to regret anything."

"I know. That word forgiveness keeps pushing into my mind and I'm not sure how I can do it, Nick. I've been bitter too long."

"Give it to—"

"God. I'm trying. Really trying."

* * *

Rona stood in the doorway of the new game room and watched Nick and Gary at opposite sides of the foosball table, spinning the rods and shouting out things that made no sense to her.

"Good shot," Nick yelled, shifting his feet, his hands darting from one handle to another.

She wandered closer, curious about this game that seemed to keep them so enraptured. Both men's focus seemed glued to the table, and though she wanted to ask questions, she kept her lips sealed. They would only accuse her of messing up a shot like they did yesterday.

She loved seeing them spend time together. It's what she'd longed for. Her heart sang as she watched.

When they'd first set up the table three days earlier, she'd thought the room needed so much work. Once she started with a little dusting and cleaning, things fell together. She'd used the furniture she'd found and dragged up a couple of extra chairs from the card table. If his friends came, they would have places to sit.

"Dead man," Gary yelled. "I got you."

"Just wait." Nick released the next ball while Rona watched the little men bat it back and forth, amazed at the speed.

"Meatball!" Nick cried.

She couldn't stop herself. "Meatball?"

Gary's voice cut off her question. "Tie score."

She wandered back against the wall and watched until Gary shouted a triumphant "Game!"

Nick's hands dropped to his side. "Okay, but next time, I'll really show you." He lapped his arm over Gary's shoulder.

"Sure you will, Dad." He patted Nick's hand resting on his shoulder.

Nick dropped his arm, and Gary dug his hand into his pocket. "Is it okay if I have some friends over on Friday? I get off work early."

"Your friends are always welcome."

Rona saw a blend of relief and pride in Nick's eyes. This is the kind of day he'd waited for and Rona found herself wanting the same—typical teenage noise in a happy home. She turned to leave the room, but Gary stopped her.

"Would you stay a minute?"

She turned back and saw his smile had faded.

Nick's grin vanished, too. "Something up, Gary?"

He glanced at Rona, then looked at his dad. "It's just something I've been wanting to tell you. It's been on my mind for a while."

Rona felt her own forehead wrinkle. "Are you sure you want me here?"

He nodded. "You wanted me to tell my dad this, and I'm ready now."

You wanted me to tell my dad this. She pushed her mind back, then remembered. Her pulse did a skip, then settled and she gave him a nod. "I'm glad."

Nick tossed his hands upward. "Okay both of you are in on this, but I'm in the dark. What's this about?"

Gary gave Rona a pleading look but she only responded with a nod. He'd started it and he had to finish.

"Rona's kept a few things from you, Dad."

Nick's face darkened. "What do you mean?" His questioning eyes pinned Rona. "Why?"

"I thought it best. Just listen to him, Nick."

Gary dug his hands more deeply into his pockets. "She found out I was smoking, and—"

"Smoking."

Rona held up her hand to quiet him. "Just listen, Nick."

"I'm sorry, Gary. Go ahead."

"I hadn't done it long, but I wanted to be like the guys. They razzed me about being a wimp. After Rona found out, I decided I'd rather be a wimp then get cancer. I'd already stopped drinking after the accident."

"Good for you, Gary." Nick moved closer and rested his hand on Gary's back.

Gary shifted away, causing Nick's hand to drop. "That's not all. Let me finish."

Rona could see him squirming, and she wanted to leave so they could have a man-to-man talk, but Gary had asked her to stay and she wanted to honor his request.

"Rona found me one day with Amy in my room. I'd sneaked her in. We were fooling around a little."

Nick's frown deepened. "Fooling around?"

"Dad." Gary looked exasperated. "We didn't go all the way, but— Do I have to give you details?"

Nick's expression relaxed, and he backed off. "No. I understand."

"After Rona made us leave the room, I realized how that must look to Jesus and how you'd feel if you knew. I know I'd done a lot of things that were sinful, but fooling around like that could lead to worse. Amy was willing, but I held back. I'm a king wimp, but it's okay."

"You're a king Christian, Gary." His tender expression rent Rona's heart.

"I've been mixed up, but I'm trying to get it all together. I figured Rona would run to you with everything, but she said she wanted me think about what I was doing and to tell you myself."

He turned to her. "Thanks for trusting me."

Rona wanted to run and wrap her arms around him. "Thanks."

He stepped forward. "Can I give you a hug?"

She opened her arms, fighting her tears, and Gary's nearly six-foot frame embraced her with a hug she'd never forget.

Chapter Fifteen

❧

Filled with the Fourth of July community pancake breakfast, Rona followed Nick through the crowds waiting for the Stars and Stripes parade. Somewhere they'd lost Gary, but Rona assumed he'd find them. To her joy, he'd gone off with some of the church teens.

She could hear the crowd cheering ahead and soon the music rose above the downtown streets of Cedarville. Rona had thought this a small town until she saw the swarms of people gathering along the streets and pulling into parking spaces around the city park.

"Dad."

Gary's voice broke through the impending noise. He edged his way to them, pushing a girl in front of him who looked familiar. "You remember Jeanie."

Jeanie. The name rang a bell and so did the face. Immediately, Rona noticed a difference between this girl and Amy. Jeanie looked pretty in striped pants and cute boatneck top, nothing clinging or revealing. "Nice to see you again. The flowers you planted look good. I noticed them when we came out of church last Sunday."

"Thanks," she said, smiling with bright eyes and giving sidelong glances to Gary. "It was fun. It's been extra fun since Gary's joined us."

He swung an arm around her neck, trying to look macho, but Rona saw the pleasure on his face.

Nick greeted Jeanie with warm welcome. "Where are your folks?" Gary gestured toward the crowd.

"They're across the street somewhere." Jeanie glanced that way, then looked back. "Gary's trying to avoid a hassle from his friends—"

"It's nothing," he said. "We'll see you later." A scowl had grown on his face.

Nick recognized Gary's frustration with Jeanie telling about Gary's problem, but he wished he could thank her. "Gary," Nick said, trying to stall him.

He'd already slipped into the crowd, but Jeanie held back. "I shouldn't have said anything."

"Tell him we'll see him at home. Drop by. We'll have burgers or something before the fireworks."

"Thanks," she said, hurrying after Gary.

Nick turned to Rona. "What was that about?"

She could guess. "I don't know for sure."

His frown deepened. "Tell me what you think."

Her stomach tightened with what she suspected. "I'm guessing it's the old buddies trying to stir up trouble. He's pulled away from the old gang. You know how kids are."

Nick looked in the direction Gary had gone. "I wish I could talk with him."

"Tonight. Jeanie will hopefully convince him to bring her over for dinner." She slipped her hand in his, amazed that it had become so easy, and gave his palm a squeeze. "Gary's a big boy. He doesn't need Daddy's protection anymore."

Nick's tense expression relaxed. "I suppose you're right, but—"

"You can protect me now."

He drew her into his arms, her back resting against his chest. "I like that offer. Now let's try to watch the parade."

How could she concentrate on the parade with her heart beating faster than the parade's drum? She did feel protected and even loved, but so often, she waited for the hammer to fall, for the bad to happen.

The past month had been a long stretch of good things happening to her—blessings. One day they would end. God seemed to want to test her faith. She'd failed Him so often. Could she succeed the next time?

With Nick's arms around her, she drew from his strength and faith. She would succeed. She had to.

Smoke from the outside grill sailed across the yard and Nick jumped from the umbrella table and rushed to it, hoping to salvage the burgers. He made it with only a few crispy edges. "I wonder what's keeping Gary."

"He'll be here. The last time we saw him, he said he and Jeanie would be here by six." She glanced at her watch. "They have another five minutes." She came to his side and wrapped her arms around him from behind. "Don't worry. He's fine."

He moved the burgers to the warming tray, lay the spatula on the grill edge and turned. "I suppose." He brushed the edge of her nose with his lips, amazed at how different life felt with Rona at his side. Still her family situation had settled in his mind, and he'd lifted it in prayer many times.

Rubbing the length of her arms, he studied the worry around her eyes. "Any decisions yet about your family?"

She tilted her head downward and shook it. "Not really, but I'm thinking about taking a couple of days and going home. I don't know how else I can resolve it until I talk with my father."

Before commenting, he'd waited to see if she mentioned her brother. "I think that's—"

Rona sucked in a breath and Nick turned around.

"Gary. What happened?" Nick eyed the swollen spot on Gary's cheek and an abrasion over his eye. He prayed it hadn't been another car accident. He'd borrowed Rona's sedan.

He sauntered forward with Jeanie clinging to his arm, and Nick figured he was trying to cover his upset. "I'm fine. You should see the other guy." He tried to smile at the old joke, but it failed.

"Fistfight?"

"It wasn't his fault, Mr. Thornton." Jeanie's expression looked tense, but beneath it, he suspected Gary was her hero.

Nick nodded. "Who was it?"

"No one you know. They were bad-mouthing."

"Me," Jeanie said.

Rona had marched to Gary's side, inspecting the wound. "It's not too bad, but you'll probably have a black eye."

"Let's get him some ice, Jeanie." Rona flagged the

girl. Though Jeanie followed Rona, she gave Gary a languishing look.

Nick loved that woman. She knew what to do to give him and Gary privacy. He closed the distance between himself and his son. "What did Jeanie mean?"

"Dad, it's okay. I did what I had to do."

"These were your friends?"

He shook his head. "Some of the old gang. They're trying to stick up for Amy since we broke up, that's all."

"What did Jeanie mean they bad-mouthed her?"

Gary waved the air. "Nothing. You know how some guys are. They called her names."

"Couldn't you just blow them off?"

"We did until they started using God's name and called her a you-know-what Jesus lover. I couldn't let them do that."

Nick rested his arm on his son's shoulder and gave it an agreeing shake. "Good for you. The old sticks-and-stones line works until they talk about our Savior."

"I wasn't going to fight. I just told him to back off and give Jeanie some respect, and one of the guys sucker punched me."

Nick felt his chest swell with pride and he understood why Jeanie had looked at him like her hero. He heard the door and saw Rona hurrying out with a plastic bag of ice and Jeanie right behind her. "Let's get that eye looked at, then we'd better eat. We want to get back to the celebration."

Rona stuck the ice against Gary's eye and he tried to duck without success.

"Hold it there for a while."

Gary shoved the bag against his cheek, eyeing Jeanie for support. "Do I have to do this?"

"Yes," Jeanie said, "listen to your moth— Rona."

Nick caught her slip and glanced at Gary to see if he had, but if so, he let it blow over.

"I'm not going back downtown tonight looking like this."

"It'll be dark for the fireworks," Rona said, her forehead wrinkling as she appeared to fight herself not to be too motherly.

Nick jumped in. "You have to go. You don't want to miss Ernie's Cruisin' Tunes and the fireworks."

Gary rolled his eyes, and Nick chuckled. He liked Ernie's music and was grateful it wasn't that hard rock noise he often heard coming from Gary's room.

Rona toweled her hair then draped the towel over the bar and looked at her image through the steamy mirror. She'd tanned and looked healthier than she had in years. Maybe it was happiness that made her feel so good.

She slipped on her robe and wandered into her apartment living room, watching the sunlight dance on the calm ripples of the lake. A breeze blew past her from the open window like a gentle kiss and she breathed in the familiar scent. Island life agreed with her. She'd become confident in using the runabout and felt free, yet secure…and safe.

She had the evening alone. Nick had a golf outing on the island. He'd taken his clothes with him for the benefit event. Rona had watched him go, wishing she could have changed her mind. She could only imagine how handsome he would look.

Tonight Gary had to work and later he was spending the evening with the youth from church. Amazing how things changed. So far no new incidents had occurred with Gary's former friends and Rona felt relieved and also amazed at how motherly she'd felt. When he'd been in the fight, she'd wanted to dive into the fray and defend him. Like Nick, she'd been so proud of his defense for Jeanie and the Lord.

Rona headed to the refrigerator and pulled out a ginger ale. She'd felt alone today, thinking about her family. She'd felt God stirring in her heart. She had to go home for a brief visit and she'd decided to tell Nick tomorrow. She knew he wanted her to go, so he would be pleased she'd made the decision.

Seeing Nick smile so often had become a gift. He and Gary's relationship had improved, at least on the outside. Rona saw fewer confrontations lately, except the typical father-son disagreements about too much noise, forgetting to do a chore or wanting to use the car. She'd decided a while ago that Gary should have his own car now that he had the job and had gotten himself together.

The can fizzed when she pulled the tab, and Rona took a long swallow of the bubbly soda. She'd need to think about dinner, but she'd become spoiled. Though she'd thought she'd spend dinners alone in her apartment, eating with the family had fallen into place and she relished in the company.

When her cell phone sang its tune, Rona's chest tightened. Since Nick was busy on Drummond, it had to be family and she could only think the worst. She located the phone and answered.

Relief washed over her hearing Nick's voice.

"I did the dumbest thing," he said.

"What?" She envisioned a car accident or a broken leg.

"I left my dress shoes home. I have everything else, but I can't go to a fancy function like this without my black shoes."

Shoes? A sigh sneaked from her. "And you want…?"

"Could you bring them to me? You won't have a problem finding the place. It's right on Maxton Bay, a short distance down the road from my resort."

So much for a quiet evening. "How soon do you need them? I just got out of the shower."

"It starts at six. You have more than an hour. I'll miss dinner if I drive back to get them."

She made a huff noise to let him know she wasn't thrilled. "Okay, where should I meet you?"

He didn't respond for a moment and she thought the call had been dropped. Finally he spoke.

"Rona, it's foolish for you to drive here and go back alone. Come for dinner. Don't argue with me on this. You might as well enjoy the evening. I rode here with John so we can ride back together."

Her heart skipped, envisioning Nick in a black suit and tie, an evening under the stars, he'd said, but reality smacked her. "Nick, I have nothing to wear even if I wanted to come."

More silence, and now she suspected a ploy. He forgot his shoes? He rode with John? "What aren't you telling me?"

"I really don't have my shoes."

Rona wanted to roll her eyes. "I'm sure." She

looked out the window at the glorious sky, soon to be filled with stars. "But what else."

"If you go into my bedroom, you'll find a dress on my bed. I'm sure it'll fit you."

A dress. No. He wouldn't. "Nick, I'm not wearing Jill's—"

"It's not Jill's."

"Then—?"

"It's yours. I bought it for you."

Her pulse skittered up her arms. "For me?"

"Please don't say no."

Tears blurred her eyes. This was the man she'd fallen in love with. Impossible maybe, but her heart didn't understand impossibilities. "I'll be there as close to six as I can."

"Thank you."

His whisper trickled to her heart.

Rona slipped from the car and smoothed the lovely fabric of her dress. She wouldn't have chosen differently, a magnificent deep ruby ankle-length gown with beaded trim that shimmered in the setting sun. She already owned black strapped pumps and a small black clutch purse, she decided to use as an evening bag.

As she approached the door, Nick stepped from the entrance. She faltered, her head swimming with nerves and with love. She'd never seen him so handsome. "You fix up nice," she said, brushing her hand along his lapel and eyeing his bow tie.

"You look amazing."

His eyes said it all and her heart swelled until she

feared it would explode. "The dress is beautiful. Thank you."

"It's more beautiful with you in it. When I saw it, I knew it was you. He touched the beads along the sleeve. The dress sparkles almost as much as your eyes."

She sensed he wanted to kiss her, and though she longed for the same, she turned toward the door, not wanting a public display.

Sliding his hand in hers, Nick guided her inside, then out to the broad patio where hors d'oeuvres and drinks were served. She accepted a glass of club soda with a twist of lime, then followed him to a group of his friends. Her hands trembled as she approached the people, but when Nick began to introduce them, her terror subsided. Two of the couples were people she knew from the church.

"Rona, it's so nice to see you. We've asked Nick over and over why he didn't bring you along to some of our events," Sherry said, casting a mischievous eye at her husband, John.

Rona managed a smile. "I'm the housekeeper, Sherry. You can't date your housekeeper."

"Phooey. Who says so? You've put a glow in Nick's eyes, and we love to see it."

Her bluntness made Rona flush. "Thanks," she mumbled, hoping most people thought her pink face was the reflection of the dress against her skin.

After they talked, Nick pulled her away to another group, and as time passed, Rona realized she knew even more people from church and from Harbor Inn. They were normal people enjoying an evening out, and she wondered why she had feared this meeting so much.

After the sun had set, spreading its glorious palette of colors over the water, Nick drew her outside to look at the stars. In the darkness and without city lights, the stars hung in the sky like a million brilliant sequins on black velvet. The beauty caught in her throat.

"The night isn't nearly as lovely as you." He slid his arm around her waist and drew her closer. "I'm sorry I tricked you into coming, but I wanted you to see that you are no different from anyone here. Some may have more money, but that doesn't make a person noble or worthy. You are amazing and, in my eyes, you're a precious gem."

She couldn't speak, but she looked at him through tears. "You've helped me to see that I'm my worst enemy."

"No. I don't want you to think that. You're—"

"I meant that in a good way. I've made the proverbial mountain out of a molehill, but let's talk about it tomorrow and just enjoy tonight." The time had come she needed to tell him the whole story. If he loved her, he would forgive her and she wanted to believe he did.

He turned his back to the others on the patio and bent down to brush her lips. "Tomorrow." He lowered his gaze and a deep chuckle turned into laughter.

"What?"

He pointed to his feet.

She looked down at his brown loafers. In her nervousness, she'd left his shoes in the car. She laughed with him as he held her in his arms.

Chapter Sixteen

$\mathbf{N}$ick wandered through the house, wondering where Rona had vanished to after church. He stepped into the dining room and gazed outside at the sun-speckled lawn, suspecting she'd gone to her apartment to change clothes. He stepped through the French doors onto the porch.

He knew they were supposed to talk today, but she'd put him off on the way to church and back, probably because Gary was there, but now he'd gone back to the mainland to work, and Nick was eager to hear what Rona had to say.

With his purpose in mind, Nick strolled from the porch stairs and down the hill to the boathouse. He climbed the steps and tapped on the door.

Rona came to the door in Capri pants and a summer top, her hair tied back in some kind of band, looking like a teenager. She tilted her head. "Hungry?"

He shook his head. "Can I come in?"

"Sure," she said, pushing open the door.

He walked in, aware of the changes she'd made to

the room by adding a few throw pillows and a new lamp. She'd moved the furniture around and he was surprised how different the room looked. "Nice job," he said, gesturing to the new additions. His gaze settled on the painting she'd won at the silent auction last night at the charity dinner. He walked over and lifted it against the wall.

"What do you think? I like it there."

Placement of the painting was the last thing he had on his mind, but he nodded. "The colors go well in the room."

"I thought so."

He shifted to a chair and sat, hoping she'd remember about the talk.

She settled onto the sofa and looked at him. "Tomorrow I'm going to visit my father."

That caused his neck to jerk upright. "You are? I'm surprised, but glad."

"I thought you would be."

"I called my cousin and she said Dad's in a hospice setting. If I'm going to do anything, it's now. I just hope I'm not too late."

He rose from the chair and moved to her side. "I hope you make it." He slipped his hand over hers, relieved, happy that she'd decided, but disappointed. He'd thought their talk might be something more about her. "That's what you wanted to tell me?"

She fell silent, then gave a quick shake of her head. He saw tears slipping to her eyes and he patted her hand, now fearing what she had to say. "Tell me. I'll understand." He sent up a prayer that God give him strength if she were saying goodbye.

"This is taking a lot of courage," she said, her voice catching in her throat. "I've known for a long time that I needed to talk with you, but I kept telling myself as long as I was your housekeeper, it didn't matter."

"You are my housekeeper."

She shook her head, "Nick, most men don't kiss the housekeeper. You and I both know—"

"That I love you."

A tear rolled down her cheek, then another, and he brushed them away with his fingertip.

"I know. At least, I hoped you did."

"I do, Rona. I didn't say it before because I wanted you to be ready when I did."

"I love you, too, Nick. You've opened my world and made me feel like a whole person again and that's why I need to tell you this. I want to be ready."

His head spun, trying to discern what she wanted to say, and he clenched his fist to control his mounting concern.

"Everything I told you about me is true, but I left out part of the story, and that's what held me back as much as believing I wasn't in your league."

He tried to speak, but she stopped him.

"Last night proved that I can fit into your world and it was then that I knew it was the full truth that had tied my hands."

"Then tell me. Please." His voice quaked when he spoke, but along with fear, he also felt confidence. The Lord forgave and Nick knew he could forgive, too, whatever it was.

She began the story with her brother. Nick had heard

some of this before, but he could tell that she was nearing the part she hadn't told him from the look on her face.

"So I agreed to drive him to pick up his money," she said. "I hated the fact that he got it from playing the numbers. No matter how far I'd pulled away from the Lord, gambling is wrong."

Nick felt frozen to the seat waiting.

"Don had me pull over to a curb and told me to wait. He'd brought a duffel bag with him, and he grabbed it, jumped out of the car and darted around a corner. I waited a few minutes and the next thing I know, Don jumps into the car with a guy chasing him and tells me to leave." She swallowed and he could see the pain in her face.

Nick's mind whirled with theories on what had happened. He pressed his hand against Rona's. "Go ahead. I'm listening."

"This is the awful part." She choked on the words, and Nick swallowed his own emotion. "I hurried off, fearing that the guy wanted to take it back. Kill him maybe. My head spun, and I looked at Don, so cool and collected, and couldn't believe what I was seeing. He clutched the bag and had me drop him off a few blocks away.

"I was glad to get rid of him, but I asked him what about my money and he said he didn't get as much as he'd expected, but he'd pay me some later. I knew I'd been duped once again with his promises. By the time I got home the police were in front of my apartment complex. The man chasing Don had gotten my license plate number. What happened didn't sink in until the police arrested me for participating in a liquor store robbery. I was devastated."

"Rona, no."

She gave one nod and broke into a sob. Nick wrapped his arms around her, trying to imagine the fear and degradation she would have felt. Her own brother. Nick's stomach churned, sick from the disgusting situation he'd heard.

He held Rona against his chest, feeling her heart pound against his shirt, her body quaking with emotion, and he didn't know what to do but hold her.

When she calmed, she drew in a ragged breath and continued. "I spent two days in jail until my dad came up with bond. They caught Don and I hired a lawyer. It took most of my savings, but I was found innocent and they sentenced Don to four years, but he could be released early for good behavior."

"Good behavior." Nick's sarcasm belted into the air. "I'm sorry, Rona, but I'm furious. Your own brother put you through that? He lied, manipulated you and set you up."

"I tried to be a good sister. I was a little older and after mom died, I wanted to be a role model for him. He used that."

"But you were innocent. You were duped. That can happen to anyone. We trust our family." The words spiked him. Jill again and his questions raced into his mind. He would probably never know, but it didn't matter anymore.

"I'm gullible. I lost my faith in people, my ability to make good decisions and my trust, especially with men. You helped me with that. You've never lied to me…except yesterday with the shoes." She managed a faint smile.

"It wasn't really a lie. I did leave my shoes at home. I didn't say I forgot them."

"I guess you didn't."

For the first time since she started her story, Rona looked into his eyes, searching and questioning, and he answered her without her speaking the words.

"It makes no difference, my sweet woman. I wish you'd told me long ago. It would have cleared up so many things and lifted the burden from you." He kissed her cheek, still damp from her tears. "Love doesn't go away because of the past. The past is like should haves. What's important is now."

"Thank you." Her lips curved in the smallest grin. "Now is important."

"And the future. After today, we can move forward. I'm the happiest man in the world."

Rona sat in the waiting room of the hospice center, her pulse galloping and perspiration beading in her palms. "I wish they'd hurry," she said to her cousin Betsy sitting beside her.

"It won't be long." Betsy patted her hand. "You just need to be prepared."

Be prepared. She'd been praying, preparing to face her father again and to offer forgiveness. The decision to visit him had been easier than the second step. Forgiveness still seemed out of reach.

Her father's violent drunkenness roared in her head. She could picture her mother flattened against the kitchen wall or prone on the floor with her father's swift kick to her side. Rona recalled trying to free her mother from his grasp and getting punched in the ribs or arms and having to hide the bruises from her teachers at school. The nightmare clamored in her head. *Lord, give me strength and Your power to forgive.*

A nurse stepped into the waiting room and looked their way. "You can see Mr. Rogers now."

"How is he?" Betsy asked.

"Resting peacefully."

Peacefully. Rona didn't know what that meant. "He's doing better?"

The woman shook her head.

"Then how much time—"

"It won't be long."

Rona felt ill. Her stomach twisted into a knot and she swallowed to keep bile from rising to her throat. She had only a short time to accomplish what the Lord had brought her here to do.

She followed Betsy down the hall and paused when she stepped into the room. Rona clung to the door frame, scanning the large area but avoiding the bed on the far side near the windows. Her cries to the Lord rang in her head. She needed strength.

Betsy turned toward her and motioned for her to come closer.

Rona took a step, feeling her knees weaken the nearer she came to the bedside, and when her cousin moved aside, Rona buried the gasp that nearly escaped.

Her father lay on the bed, gaunt and ashen. His strong arms, which had wreaked such havoc, lay at his sides, the skin loose and white. How long had it been since she'd seen her father? Even before the horrible event with Don, she'd avoided her father for at least two years. Had four years passed since she'd seen him?

Shame flooded her. God expected believers to reach out to the enemy, to turn the other cheek, to be light in the darkness. She hadn't offered a dim spark to heal the wounds. She'd allowed hurt and fear to sink her into an abyss of private misery. A praise rose in her heart, a praise to God for His goodness and to the gift of Nick who'd helped her see the light.

"Dad." Her whisper pierced the silence.

He didn't move, but she saw his shallow, uneven gasps ruffle the sheet.

"Dad. It's Rona."

His lids fluttered, then his eyes opened.

Rona looked into his glassy stare.

"Rona."

The single word tore through her heart. Pity, sorrow and remorse overwhelmed her. "I'm sorry I haven't been to see you."

He didn't speak yet seemed to understand. "I messed up, Rona." He'd appeared to run out of air.

"Don't talk. It's okay."

"I'm sorry." His words were a gasp.

Sorry. One small word to cover a mountain of sin. Yet that's all God expected to grant forgiveness.

Rona tried to form the words, but her tongue felt frozen. *Lord, be with me.* She opened her mouth, freeing her tongue and fighting the lump in her throat. "Dad, I forgive you."

Dumbfounded, Rona watched a tear roll from the corner of his eye and drip to the pillow. Without holding back, she touched her father's hand, a hand she had never touched since she could remember, except to fend away his drunken blows. His cold fingers lay beneath her palm as words rushed from her mouth. "I pray God forgives you, too."

His gaze connected with hers, this time clear and focused, before his eyes closed again. "Forgive me, Lord," he whispered.

Her heart thundered and she heard Betsy's quiet gasp. Rona felt his hand slide from hers, the sheet sank with her father's final rattle of breath. Rona buried her face in her hands and wept.

Betsy's arm slid over her shoulders, guiding her away from the bed, while she flagged the nurse to take over.

The nurse stepped closer and pulled the curtain.

"It's over, Rona." She patted her arm. "I'm astounded. I didn't know your father was a believer."

Getting a grip on herself, Rona sank into a chair, facing the curtain, then wiped her eyes. "I didn't, either. Maybe he wasn't, but God touched him today."

"He was waiting for you, Rona. I really think he lived to see you again so he could say he was sorry."

Rona lifted her head, pondering the possibility. A hand touched her shoulder and she jolted upward.

"If it isn't my big sister."

Bile rose before she could control it. "Don. You're too late."

"Late?" His eyes narrowed.

"He's gone."

He eyed the pulled curtain. "Gone where?"

Betsy's voice broke in. "He died, Don, a few minutes ago."

"Why that old buzzard. I've been sitting here for two days, waiting for him to go."

Betsy grunted. "You were here about two hours the past two days."

Rona smelled the liquor on Don's breath and saw the drugged gaze in his eyes. Prison had accomplished nothing with Don. She wanted to beat her fists against his chest.

"So how are things going, sis? Where are you living now?"

"Far away, and things are fine."

"Don't you want to know about me?"

He tried to chuck her under the chin, but she batted his hand away. "You're still a drunk and a druggy. I know that."

"Witch." He staggered away and plopped into a nearby chair.

A seed of fear sank into Rona's consciousness. Don would do what he could to ruin her life and she had no idea why. She'd tried to be a good sister. Her mind went back, unable to find an answer.

Betsy's voice cut into her thoughts. "Rona, you'll stay for the funeral, won't you?"

Rona focused on her. "Yes, then I'll go back up—"

"Up. Up north. Interesting." Don's voice sliced through her.

Rona wanted to start again, to replay the moment and correct her slip. She drew up her shoulders, knowing that she couldn't hide forever. Don would find her.

Nick paced the family room, then strode to the dining room and looked out toward the water. Gary had promised to be back by eight and though the sun hadn't sunk beneath the lake, he still worried about him boating at night in the small runabout.

He'd called the church earlier and received no answer. He'd thought Gary had gone to a youth event, but he might have been wrong. His mind had been on Rona, and he recalled only nodding and saying, "Back by eight." Gary had agreed.

By eight-thirty, he'd called the pastor and learned there had been no youth activity that evening. Now his last hope was Jeanie's. He located the church directory and found the phone number. He hated to be a worried father. Gary had been doing so well, but that was the problem. Gary had promised to be home by eight. He had to start early at the restaurant tomorrow morning.

He punched in the numbers and waited. "Mrs. Rasmussen, this is Nick Thornton. Is Gary there?"

"I've been waiting for them," she said, her voice concerned. "Gary said they'd be back about seven."

Seven. That would have given Gary enough time to get home by eight. His stomach tightened. "Do you know where they were headed?"

"Gary said it was a surprise, but Jeanie took her swimsuit and a picnic lunch. Just a couple of sandwiches and fruit."

Surprise. Picnic. Swimming. Fear caught in Nick's throat. "Government Island. I wonder if that's where they went."

"Way over there?"

"I'll take the speedboat and go over. I'll call you if I find anything."

Nick quaked with panic as he tucked his cell phone into his pocket and darted from the house. He revved the boat and swung out, creating a wake in a no-wake area as he raced toward Marquette Bay. Taking the route around Marquette put him in open water where he could open the throttle.

He turned on his lights in the dusky evening. The water seemed rough and he looked into the sky to see evidence of a storm brewing. Cumulus clouds billowed overhead, their bottoms slate gray and hinting of rain. He sent up a prayer, raising his speed as he whipped around Coves Point into the open water. Once past Fuyard Point he had a straight shot to Government Island.

Darkness lowered over the water and drops of rain dotted his windshield. He strained the boat to its limit, the waves smacking the hull and lifting him upward. Why had Gary gone to that beach? He could have chosen so many safer ones, but Nick thought about his disappointing day with Amy when he swam alone and didn't eat his lunch, and Nick realized he wanted the perfect picnic. He'd made the decision without looking at the sky and seeing the storm.

Storms had a way of sneaking up on people. He thought of his own struggles after Jill died and his year of torment with Gary's belligerence. God had been good and calmed his storms. Today God could do the same.

His thoughts sailed to Rona and the funeral. When she called, he'd heard the stress in her voice, but he'd rejoiced when she shared the story of forgiveness and the hope for her father's eternal life in heaven. Nick had agreed. Her father's last dying breath calling to the Lord had been a good sign. Nick could only wish such hopes for Rona's brother. The man sounded psychotic and evil.

Government Island loomed ahead, its gray outline in the growing darkness. He veered and headed toward the beach and his heart rose to his throat when he saw a boat drifting in the current. His boat. Gary's boat— empty.

Nick pulled aside, grasped the ropes and pulled the boat behind him, then tied it. This would slow him, but his hopes rose. If the boat drifted away in the current, then God willing Gary and Jeanie were stranded on the island and were safe.

He headed around the point toward the picnic area, slowed the boat and called. He tried to listen above the hum of his motor. Through the rain, he saw two forms racing toward the beach, their hands waving in the air.

"Thank you, Lord," Nick cried out. He glided close to shore while the teens climbed on board, shivering in the cooler night air.

"Dad, I'm—"

"No need. Accidents happen." He clutched the two in his arms, overcome with relief.

Accidents happen. The words flooded him with calm. Accidents. Jill's death had been an accident. Finally, he knew this with certainty.

Nick dug into the storage beneath the seats, pulled out a blanket and tossed it to them. "Now, let's get home."

Chapter Seventeen

"When's Rona coming back?" Gary stood in the doorway of the family room and stretched.

"Sometime today. She called early this morning and said she would probably leave soon, so I'd expect her around dinnertime."

Gary plopped onto the sofa, his face strained from the accident the day before, and Nick knew he regretted his carelessness in mooring the boat. "Dad, I'm sorry about—"

Nick held up his hand. "You don't have to say another word. I know you're sorry." Gary had apologized to him and to Jeanie's parents over and over. Lessons had to be learned the hard way sometimes.

Gary leaned forward, his head lowered. "I'm not apologizing about the accident again."

His words swept over Nick, and he studied his son's face.

"I'm sorry about everything since Mom died." He stood up and shoved his hands in his pockets. "Yesterday opened my eyes."

Nick held his breath.

"Like you said, accidents happen and—" His voice choked and Gary hesitated, Nick realized, to gain composure.

Nick nodded, not wanting to interrupt.

"I never told you this, but when Mom died, I'd begun to wonder why. I was thirteen and somehow I'd convinced myself she wanted to die because I was a bad person."

"Gary, you were never—"

"You don't know, Dad."

Know what? Nick struggle to maintain his cool.

"When I'd spotted Mom drinking, I attacked her. I told her I'd tell you. She said it was medicine. That she'd been feeling sick. I knew that was bologna, but I wondered what was really wrong. You were so busy working. You had businesses, I know, but when you're a kid, you want everyone to focus on you and not work. I felt Mom falling apart and my dad totally oblivious."

"I know that now. I do."

"I still thought it had to do with me. Neither one of you wanted to spend time with me. You were both caught up in your own worlds. So when Mom died, I thought it was an escape from me. Then I couldn't bear it anymore. and decided to blame you, because I couldn't stand—"

Nick was on his feet and wrapping his arms around his son. "Gary, I've been blaming myself. I've feared that your mom was so unhappy that she took…that she wanted to die. We were having problems."

"I know you were. She didn't like your working long hours, either. But it wasn't your fault, Dad. Mom told me she loved you, but she didn't love herself."

Nick felt the floor drop beneath him as if plunging to his death in an elevator. He clung to Gary to keep his balance, fearing he'd frighten his son. "Your mom said that?"

"I accused her of hating both of us, and she said she loved us with all her heart. She just hated herself. But why?"

Overtaken by Gary's words, Nick couldn't speak.

"Why, Dad?"

"I don't know. Your mom wanted lots of things and the more I worked to please her the more I didn't please her. Sometimes people think material things will make them happy when it's something missing inside them. I loved your mom and didn't know what was wrong. She'd had a bad time with her sister. They weren't close, but why? Your mom didn't talk much about that, so I never knew."

"I saw what happened."

Nick drew back and clasped Gary's shoulders. "You saw the accident?"

He nodded, tears growing in his eyes. "Another boat was passing us on your side. You'd turned the other way to look at Mom and didn't see it. I think Mom raised her hand to wave and she was swung to the left. The wake of the boat pushed her farther left. The raft looked like it appeared out of nowhere."

Nick swallowed his emotion, grateful for the truth. "I saw the raft and I saw the boat, Gary. I was trying to stay away from both."

"Then you did all you could. Mom didn't want to die. It was an accident."

He'd said that to himself, but validation covered

Nick like a healing balm. He drew Gary into an embrace and they stood there a long time without saying anything else.

Rona loved the feel of Nick's hand in hers, his strong fingers wrapped around her palm giving her a sense of security and love. He'd said he loved her and Rona believed every word.

Since she'd arrived home, a weight had lifted from her shoulders. Forgiveness opened her and she felt renewed after ridding herself of the bitterness. Her only baggage now was Don, and she believed that only God could save him from damnation.

"You're thoughtful." Nick's voice drew her from her thoughts. "Ready to go or do you want to stay? We have time."

Rona looked at the temporary tents filled with art displays and food for Hessel's Music and Art Dockside annual event. Surrounded by music, people lingered, tempted to spend their money on new artworks and crafts. She'd purchased a candleholder made from a tree branch still covered with bark. With a thick candle, it would add a nice touch to a window table in her apartment.

She blocked the sun from her eyes and gazed at Nick. "What time's the reservation?"

"Not until six-thirty, but we'll have to leave by five-thirty, I suppose, between the drive and ferry."

Excited, she looked forward to another evening at Bayside Dining, the place Nick had tricked her into attending that charity dinner.

Eyeing her watch, Rona calculated how long it

would take her to get ready. She'd purchased a dress for the evening without telling Nick and looked forward to surprising him. This one was a deep teal calf-length number with lovely lace crochet inserts on the neck and sleeve. "It's close to three-thirty. Why don't we go home?" Go home. The words sounded wonderful.

Nick shifted his hand up her arm and wrapped it around her shoulders. "Sounds good to me."

Rona had gotten used to the ride and the time passed more quickly than when she first experienced the trip to Nick's house. The day seemed a year ago but it had just been a couple of months. Nick nosed between the docks and she helped tie the boat, then kissed him goodbye as she hurried up the stairs to her apartment, anxious to take a shower and slip into her new dress.

Watching Nick from the landing, Rona pulled open the door and stepped inside.

"Hi, sis."

Her heart exploded. "What are you doing here? How did you find me?"

"You left telltale hints. I think you wanted me to look for you."

A million questions swam in her head. "How did you get in here? Where's your boat?"

"I'm smart enough not to dock here and I opened the door and walked in. It wasn't locked."

Maybe this was her fear about leaving the door unlocked.

"And you must know, sis, that a small town gives away a lot of free information."

Rona wanted to knock the smug look from his face.

"When you mentioned up north, I remembered

Hessel. You used to visit here with one of your little friends. Remember?"

She didn't give him the pleasure of a nod.

"So I dropped by the inn there in the bay and asked a few questions. People were so happy to tell me how you'd worked there and then got a housekeeping job with a rich man who apparently fell in love with you. Too bad he doesn't know about your little escape in Detroit."

"He knows, Don. I told him."

"Really."

His doubt-filled voice crept up her spine. "Please leave, Don. I have nothing to give you anymore."

"But your rich boyfriend might, to have your loving brother vanish."

"Rona?" Nick's voice jolted from the speaker.

Don rose from the chair and crossed to her, his finger on his lips. "Don't say a word," he whispered.

She backed away from the intercom, knowing that if she didn't answer Nick would be there in a flash. "Okay."

"Rona? What's wrong?" Nick's voice sang out again.

Don grasped her arm. "Answer it, but be fast."

Panic swallowed her as she tried to think of a way to signal him. No matter what she might say Don would catch on. "I'm here. I was getting ready to shower."

Nick's voice sailed to her. "We'll need to leave earlier than I said. I forgot I need to stop at John's for a minute."

"No problem. I'll be ready." She lifted her finger to turn off the intercom, but left it pressed in.

"Get away from that thing," Don said, pushing his fingers into her forearm and forcing her away from it.

"You're hurting me."

He dropped his hand. "Here's my plan. Your boyfriend has loot. Look at this place. I hear he has a resort and a construction business. Those people in town were so pleased to tell your favorite brother all the tidbits they could."

"I don't know anything about Nick's money. I'm the housekeeper."

He snorted. "Not what I see. You're his little plaything."

She clenched her fist not to backhand him. *Lord, give me wisdom.*

"I just need a little money to get a new start. Fifty thousand would be good." He grasped her arm again and sank his thumb into her muscle. She flinched with the pain.

"Make up a story. You need to help an old friend. Anything. He'll give it to you."

The door swung open and Nick charged into the room, his eyes flashing with disgust. "Take your hands off her."

He bound to Don's side and jerked him away. "You have no business here and I wouldn't give you a penny." He swung his arm toward the door. "Get out and don't come back."

"What do you think the townspeople will think when I give them the lowdown on Rona's wriggling out of a robbery."

"They'll laugh you out of town, Don. People here know Rona and they care about her. You're a stranger. They won't listen to your lies."

Don moved toward the door, then faltered. "Look. Just give me a few bucks. I need to get some people off my back."

Rona clutched Nick's arm. "And you'll need more people off your back next week, Don. Then the next. It's unending. Change. Get a job. That's what Mom would want for you."

"Mom cared nothing about me. You were the golden girl."

"I'm sorry," Rona said. "I can't change that, but you can change. It takes work. The only thing I can do for you is pray."

"Pray!" His scoff echoed in Rona's ears.

Nick moved toward him. "If you come around here again, I'll have the police cart your sorry carcass out of here. This isn't a threat. It's a warning. I have no use for you."

"You'll be sorry," Don screamed as he pushed open the door and darted down the stairs.

"I'm so sorry," Rona said, falling into Nick's arms. "I've feared this might happen and—"

"Shhh. He can't hurt you any longer. I'm sorry I didn't try to reason with him."

"You can't reason with Don. I've tried."

Nick cuddled her in his arms until she had calmed. She moved away to get a tissue.

He motioned to the intercom. "Great thinking. I would never have known." He pushed the off button.

"I hoped you'd hear." She hiccuped another sob.

Nick drew her into his arms again. "Let's cancel dinner tonight. I want this to be—"

"No, Nick. I'm so sorry about Don. He ruined—"

He shook his head. "I want the night to be special. I'll make the reservations for next weekend. It's best. I promise."

Rona trembled with her ragged nerves. "Okay." This was no night to enjoy a romantic dinner.

Nick gave her a final squeeze, then headed for the door. "Come up to the house when you're dressed."

Rona listened to his footsteps on the stairs and when they were gone, she closed the door and locked it.

Rona's mind had wandered for the past two days since she'd found Don in her apartment. When would he show up again to ruin her life? He always did in one way or another. She didn't know how to pray for him anymore, but she continued to try. God knew her heart and that's what counted.

Nick had changed their reservation to next Saturday and it had been a wise decision. Sunday after Don had charged off, she'd felt as if a hammer had struck her between the eyes. The headache vanished on Monday, replaced by apprehension. Don had made threats and he usually carried them out.

She wiped the kitchen counter, still awed by Nick's gorgeous home. She loved every nook and cranny. With the kitchen spotless, Rona headed to the hallway and grabbed the vacuum cleaner. The family room wasn't on her schedule, but Gary and his friends had tracked in clumps of grass from the yard.

The house sounded wonderful with the noise of teens laughing and yelling from the game room. She never thought she would say she loved noise, but it filled her with a sense of belonging, a wonderful sensation she'd missed much of her life.

As she started the vacuum cleaner, she felt her pocket vibrate. She snapped off the machine and pulled out her cell phone. "Hi," she said, waiting to hear Nick's voice.

"This is Sergeant Dickson of the Sault Ste. Marie police department."

Police? A pain shot through her stomach.

"We found your phone number in the pocket of a Don Rogers. Do you know this man?"

She struggled for breath. "Yes, he's my brother. What's wrong? What has he done now?"

"Are you Miss Rogers?"

"I'm Rona Meyers."

"I'm sorry, but…your brother was killed while attempting to rob a liquor store."

"No," she whispered, as tears rolled from her eyes. Don's life hung before her, sending a deep ache in her heart. Don had destroyed his life with alcohol and drugs. "Did he hurt anyone?"

"No, but we need you or another family member to come here and identify the body."

She brushed away her tears with trembling hands as she grasped a pencil and paper. "I'll be there. Could you give me directions?"

When she'd disconnected, Rona stood a moment, letting the sergeant's message sink in. Then she looked heavenward. Was this the only way?

Clutching her cell phone in her shaking palm, she punched in Nick's number. She needed Nick. He would go with her. She couldn't do this alone.

When she heard his voice, peace washed over her.

Rona gazed out the windows at the star-studded sky. The past week had been stressful, but she'd been

able to give it to the Lord. He promised to carry her
burdens and He had done that.

Nick's hand touched hers and she lifted her eyes,
knowing she'd been quiet too long. "Have I told you
how beautiful you are?"

She nodded, remembering the look on his face
when he saw her in the new dress.

"You're ravishing."

"You're pretty handsome yourself."

He grinned. "Have I told you that I love you?"

"Not in the last ten minutes."

"Then it's time I tell you again, but this time with
some positive action."

"Positive action?" Her hand flew to her lacy neck-
line. "You're not going to kiss me in public."

"That sounds like a great idea, but we'll save the
kiss for later." He lifted his other hand and slid a black
velvet box onto the table.

Rona's heart skipped. "Nick."

"Open it."

She lifted it and raised the lid. Inside, the most
beautiful diamond she'd ever seen winked at her in the
dim lights, its fire of blue and red shooting color like
fireworks in her heart. "It's gorgeous."

"I'd hoped you'd like it. I bought it downstate and
when John was making a trip to Traverse City, I asked
him to pick it up for me. I wanted it for tonight."

"So that's why you said we had to stop there last
week?"

He grinned. "I'm sorry. John and Sherry knew
before you did, but they were so excited."

Rona didn't care. They'd become good friends. She

lifted the ring from the satin and held it in her fingers, the diamond so large she couldn't believe it was hers. "What about Gary? Does he know?"

"He's your biggest fan."

"My fan?"

"He asked me why I took so long. The kid's wise for sixteen."

"Nearly seventeen. His birthday's in a few days."

"Rona, you've made our life so complete. You came into our lives with your energy and amazing smile and straightened us out."

"I didn't straighten you out. You did lots of work with God's help. I watched you and Gary come together and I loved every minute of healing. Both of you came to grips with the problems."

He squeezed her hand. "But I think you were the catalyst."

Her heart soared. "I'm glad."

"Let's go outside for a minute."

Rona reached for the box, but Nick took the diamond from her hand, then caught her arm and steered her onto the patio.

Under the summer sky, she turned to face him as he lifted her hand and slipped the ring onto her finger. A perfect fit. Nick lifted her hand and kissed it, then drew her closer and lowered his lips to hers. She tasted his sweetness, the depth of his love flowed from him to her heart and the kiss held promises she could only imagine. A life with the man she loved. A life free from fear. Her mind soared with the new life that awaited them.

Chapter Eighteen

Saturday, September 15

"I now pronounce you man and wife. You may kiss the bride." Pastor Al's voice resounded in Nick's ears. He'd waited so long to hear those words.

Nick caressed Rona's cheek, gazing at her shining face, a face that had intrigued him from the moment he'd laid eyes on her at the inn. Today her eyes told him everything he needed to know. She loved him with her whole heart. He lowered his mouth to hers, their lips now feeling at home together, a soft touch that deepened for a moment before separating.

They smiled, then turned to face their friends in their family room, the perfect place for the perfect wedding. A cheer went up from those gathered and a rush of guests came toward them, arms open wide to embrace them.

Betsy wiped her eyes and clutched Rona's bouquet. Gary stood beside them, smiling, and Nick had been so pleased he'd chosen his son to be the best man.

"Toss the bouquet," someone called.

Rona laughed and took the bouquet from Betsy. She turned and flung it over her head and Nick saw Mandy grasp the flowers above her head. Her date grinned at her and he wondered if it were a serious relationship. Love happens when you least expect it.

Jeanie came up with her parents and gave Nick a hug, then turned to Rona. "I can call you Mrs. Thornton now."

"You can, Jeanie," Rona said, as if she'd just realized it. She embraced the girl, and then turned to Gary. "I'm proud to have you as a stepson, Gary."

"Let's just say son," he said, kissing her on the cheek. "You've been a great mom to me."

Tears billowed in Rona's eyes and Nick slipped his arm around her waist, feeling the silky fabric beneath his fingers, the soft beige gown with lace and beads. When he'd seen her for the first time that day, happiness had filled every pore.

Nick felt blessed with Gary's amazing change, so blessed that on his last birthday, he'd given Gary a car as a surprise, a car Rona had bugged him about for months.

"Let's eat," Nick said, motioning their guests toward the French doors.

Shirley Bailey came forward, a coy grin on her wrinkled face. Nick had finally met her one day in town, and he liked her. She gave him a handshake, then took Rona's hand in hers. "Didn't I tell you?"

Rona's face filled with question. "Tell me what?"

"God knew what He was doing. He had His plan."

Rona shook her head and gave Nick a grin. "Shirley told me you and I were going to get together the second time I visited her." She turned to Shirley. "Or was it the first?"

"This old mind can barely remember the time of day, but I did feel it in my heart. You both look so happy together. I'll keep your family in my prayers."

Family. Nick loved the sound of that word.

Shirley moved away and, one by one, others wished them happiness, then headed outside until Rona and Nick stood alone for a moment.

He drew her to him. "I can't say it enough. You fill me with such joy."

"I love you," she whispered, her voice catching with emotion. She brushed tears from her eyes. "Now I suppose you expect me to move into the house."

He laughed at her unexpected silliness. "I suppose, but if you don't want to—"

She pressed her finger to his lips. "Nothing could keep me away."

"That's what I want to hear," he said, when she lowered her hand. He drew her closer. "Before we go out to our guests, I want to tell you what a blessing you are. You've given me so much, especially the family that's been in my heart."

"And the family I never had."

He wove his fingers through hers and they stepped outside into a new day and a new life together.

Dear Reader,

I hope you enjoyed spending time in the beautiful Les Cheneaux area of Michigan. Researching this book was a delight and I'm so pleased I could share a little of its charm with you and introduce you to Rona and Nick, two people struggling with their pasts.

Each of us have part of our pasts we would like to erase, things we've said or done that have hurt others or ourselves. Christians do not escape sin or troubles and I hope this story has helped you to know that the past is gone and what's important is now…and the future.

God has promised us forgiveness and His love when we follow Him and call on His name. Jesus said in Matthew 11:28, "Come to Me, all you who are weary and burdened, and I will give you rest." I pray you rest in the Lord's promises and let His light shine in you.

Blessings always,

Gail Gaymer Martin

QUESTIONS FOR DISCUSSION

1. Along with the guilt of being duped by her brother, Rona felt ashamed of her family. In what way have you experienced this in your own life?

2. Nick felt responsible for his wife's death. Why did he feel responsible? What caused him to change his mind?

3. Raising teenagers is a challenge to many parents. What do you believe made a difference in Nick and Gary's relationship?

4. Though Shirley Bailey was a minor character, what purpose did she serve in this story? Do you know anyone in your own life that reminds you of the elderly woman?

5. Teenagers struggle with the "world" while clinging to their faith. Where did Gary go wrong and what helped him to return to the right path with the Lord?

6. Nick struggles with the concept of being a family. Why does he do this? What does the word *family* mean to you? What was Nick searching for when he longed for the sense of family?

7. Though Rona was a beautiful woman in Nick's eyes, what seemed more important to him than her

looks? Is this kind of thinking important for a successful relationship? Why or why not?

8. Have you ever visited an island that required a ferry trip to and from the mainland? What are the pros and cons of island life?

9. Rona mentioned how news seems to travel quickly in small towns. Do you agree with that or do you think small towns are the same as any other town? Why or why not?

10. In what way do you think the Bible verse theme Deuteronomy 4:9 fits this story?

"Welcome to the family, Briton," said one of Olaf's men in a mocking voice. "We look forward to the presence of a woman at our hall."

Bronwen grasped her tunic and yanked it from the Viking's thick fingers. As she stepped away from the table, she heard the drunken laughter of the barbarians behind her. How could her father have betrothed her to the old Viking?

Running down the stone steps toward the heavy oak door that led outside the keep, Bronwen gathered her mantle about her. She ordered the doorman to open the door, and he did so reluctantly, pressing her to carry a torch. But Bronwen pushed past him and fled into the darkness.

Dashing down the steep, pebbled hill toward the beach, she felt the frozen ground give way to sand. She threw off her veil and circlet and kicked away her shoes.

Racing alongside the pounding surf, she felt hot tears of anger and shame well up and stream down her

cheeks. With no concern for her safety, Bronwen ran
and ran, her long braids streaming behind her, falling
loose, drifting like a tattered black flag.

Blinded with weeping, she did not see the dark
form that loomed suddenly in her path and stopped
dead her headlong sprint. Bronwen shrieked in surprise and fear as iron arms pinned her, and a heavy
cloak threatened to suffocate her.

"Release me!" she cried. "Guard! Guard, help me!"

"Hush, my lady." A deep voice emanated from the
darkness. "I mean you no harm. What demon drives
you to run so madly in the night without fear for
your safety?"

"Release me, villain! I am the daughter—"

"I shall hold you until you calm yourself. We had
heard there were witches in Amounderness, but I had
not thought to meet one so openly."

Still held in the man's arms, Bronwen drew back
and peered up at the hooded figure. "You! You are the
man who spied on our feast. Release me at once or I
shall call the guard upon you."

The man chuckled at this and turned toward his
companions, who stood in a group nearby. Bronwen
caught hold of the back of his hood and jerked it down
to reveal a head of glossy raven curls. But the man's
face was shrouded in darkness yet, and as he looked
at her, she could not read his expression.

"So you are the blessed bride-to-be." He pulled the
hood back over his head. "Your father has paired you
with an interesting choice."

Relieved that her captor did not appear to be a high-
wayman, she sagged from his warm hands onto the

wet sand. "Please leave me here alone. I need peace to think. Go on your way."

The tall stranger shrugged off his outer mantle and wrapped it around her shoulders. "Why did your father betroth you thus to the aged Viking?" he asked.

"For one purported to be a spy, you know precious little about Amounderness. But I shall tell you, as it is all common knowledge."

She pulled the cloak tightly about her, reveling in its warmth. "Our land, Amounderness, once was Briton territory. Olaf Lothbrok, my betrothed, came here as a youth when the Viking invasions had nearly subsided. He took the lands directly to the south of Rossall Hall from their Briton lord. Then, of course, the Normans came, and Amounderness was pillaged by William the Conqueror's army."

The man squatted on the sand beside Bronwen. He listened with obvious interest as she continued the familiar tale. "When William took an account of Amounderness in his Doomsday Book, he recorded no remaining lords and few people at all. But he did not know the Britons. Slowly, we crept out of hiding and returned to our halls. My father's family reoccupied Rossall Hall. And there we live, as we should, watching over our serfs as they fish and grow their meager crops. Indeed, there is not much here for the greedy Normans to want, if they are the ones for whom you spy."

Unwilling to continue speaking when her heart was so heavy, Bronwen stood and turned toward the sea. The traveler rose beside her and touched her arm. "Olaf Lothbrok's lands—together with your father's—

will reunite most of Amounderness. A clever plan. Your sister's future husband holds the rest of the adjoining lands, I understand."

"You've done your work, sir. Your lord will be pleased. Who is he—some land-hungry Scottish baron? Or have you forgotten that King Stephen gave Amounderness to the Scots as a trade for their support in his war with Matilda? I certainly hope your lord is not a Norman. He would be so disappointed to learn he has no legal rights here. Now, if you will excuse me?"

Bronwen turned and began walking back along the beach toward Rossall Hall. She felt better for her run, and somehow her father's plan did not seem so farfetched anymore. Distant lights twinkled through the fog that was rolling in from the west and she suddenly realized what a long way she had come.

"My lady," the stranger's voice called out behind her.

Bronwen kept walking, unwilling to face again the one who had seen her in her humiliation. She did not care what he reported to his master.

"My lady, you have a bit of a walk ahead of you." The traveler strode forward to join her. "Perhaps I should accompany you to your destination."

"You leave me no choice, I see."

"I am not one to compromise myself, dear lady. I follow the path God has set before me and none other."

"And just who are you?"

"I am called Jacques."

"French. A Norman, as I had suspected."

The man chuckled. "Not nearly as Norman as you are Briton."

As they approached the fortress, Bronwen could see

that the guests had not yet begun to disperse. Perhaps no one had missed her and she could slip quietly into bed beside Gildan.

She turned to go, but he took her arm and studied her face in the moonlight. Then, gently, he drew her into the folds of his hooded cloak. "Perhaps the bride would like the memory of a younger man's embrace to warm her," he whispered.

Astonished, Bronwen attempted to remove his arms from around her waist. But she could not escape his lips as they found her own. The kiss was soft and warm, melting away her resistance like the sun upon the snow. Before she had time to react, he was striding back down the beach.

Bronwen stood stunned for a moment, clutching his woolen mantle about her. Suddenly she cried out, "Wait, Jacques! Your mantle!"

The dark one turned to her. "Keep it for now," he shouted into the wind. "I shall ask for it when we meet again."

*Don't miss this deeply moving
Love Inspired Historical story about
a medieval lady who finds strength in God
to save her family legacy—
and open her heart to love.*

*THE BRITON
by Catherine Palmer
available February 2008*

*And also look for
HOMESPUN BRIDE
by Jillian Hart,
where a Montana woman discovers that
love is the greatest blessing of all.*

REQUEST YOUR FREE BOOKS!

2 FREE INSPIRATIONAL NOVELS
PLUS 2
FREE
MYSTERY GIFTS

Love Inspired

YES! Please send me 2 FREE Love Inspired® novels and my 2 FREE mystery gifts. After receiving them, if I don't wish to receive any more books, I can return the shipping statement marked "cancel." If I don't cancel, I will receive 4 brand-new novels every month and be billed just $3.99 per book in the U.S., or $4.74 per book in Canada, plus 25¢ shipping and handling per book and applicable taxes, if any*. That's a savings of 20% off the cover price! I understand that accepting the 2 free books and gifts places me under no obligation to buy anything. I can always return a shipment and cancel at any time. Even if I never buy another book from Steeple Hill, the two free books and gifts are mine to keep forever.

113 IDN EF26   313 IDN EF27

Name _____ (PLEASE PRINT) _____

Address _____ Apt. # _____

City _____ State/Prov. _____ Zip/Postal Code _____

Signature (if under 18, a parent or guardian must sign) _____

Order online at www.LoveInspiredBooks.com
Or mail to Steeple Hill Reader Service™:
IN U.S.A.: P.O. Box 1867, Buffalo, NY 14240-1867
IN CANADA: P.O. Box 609, Fort Erie, Ontario L2A 5X3

Not valid to current Love Inspired subscribers.

Want to try two free books from another series?
Call 1-800-873-8635 or visit www.morefreebooks.com

* Terms and prices subject to change without notice. NY residents add applicable sales tax. Canadian residents will be charged applicable provincial taxes and GST. This offer is limited to one order per household. All orders subject to approval. Credit or debit balances in a customer's account(s) may be offset by any other outstanding balance owed by or to the customer. Please allow 4 to 6 weeks for delivery.

Your Privacy: Steeple Hill is committed to protecting your privacy. Our Privacy Policy is available online at www.eHarlequin.com or upon request from the Reader Service. From time to time we make our lists of customers available to reputable firms who may have a product or service of interest to you. If you would prefer we not share your name and address, please check here. ☐

LIREG07

INTRODUCING

Love Inspired.

HISTORICAL

A NEW TWO-BOOK SERIES.

Every month, acclaimed
inspirational authors
will bring you engaging stories
rich with romance, adventure
and faith set in a variety
of vivid historical times.

History begins on **February 12**
wherever you buy books.

Steeple
Hill®

www.SteepleHill.com

TITLES AVAILABLE NEXT MONTH

Don't miss these four stories in February

A DREAM TO SHARE by Irene Hannon
Heartland Homecoming
Mark Campbell was in Missouri to convince Abby Warner to sell her family's newspaper to his conglomerate. He didn't want to spend any more time in the one-stoplight town than he had to. But the feisty newswoman brought out feelings in Mark that were front-page worthy.

HEALING TIDES by Lois Richer
Pennies from Heaven
Doctors aren't supposed to get attached to patients, yet GloryAnn Cranbrook couldn't help falling for one sick little boy. He needed a procedure only her boss, Dr. Jared Steele, could perform. So why wouldn't he do it? It was up to GloryAnn to change his mind—and his heart.

FOUR LITTLE BLESSINGS by Merrillee Whren
The four little noisemakers who'd moved next door to Wade Dalton came with a bonus: their beautiful aunt. Wade was attracted to the chaos that surrounded them, though he had a secret that could keep them all apart. Something the four little blessings weren't about to let happen.

HER UNLIKELY FAMILY by Missy Tippens
Her calling was to help teenage runaways. But when the handsome, uptight uncle of her newest girl showed up, Josie Miller knew she was in over her head. Michael Throckmorton didn't know the first thing about parenting. Maybe she could help them all become a family.

LICNM0108